DARK
TREASURES

SERGIO GOMEZ

Edited by: David Yost

Cover design by: Teddi Black

For Laura

"the roses have wilted
the violets are dead,
the demons go
round and round in my head."
——Anonymous Poem

TABLE OF CONTENTS

Introduction

In between the first draft and the second draft of something, I like to step away from the story. This is something I learned from Stephen King's book *On Writing,* and is probably some of the most useful and effective advice I'd ever read.

In this interval of time, the writer can separate himself from the emotional attachment to the world and characters he just finished creating, an important step in the process because it lets him see the story as an outsider when he finally returns to it.

I bring this up because that's how "Pills" came to be. I was in between drafts of a novel and needed a new project to fill in that waiting period. I started writing the story, and initially my plan was to sell it to a magazine or website, but once I got to about the café scene I realized I was pouring everything I had into this. The story and characters began to consume me the same way any of my novels have done in the past.

This brewed an idea, and I thought, hey, if I can write at least 7 more stories as strong as *Pills*, I could probably put them together and release them in a collection. So, that's exactly what I did. Well, to be honest, I wrote more than seven; I wrote maybe fifteen stories all together. Most of them won't ever see the light of day, and others just didn't work well with the overall theme of the anthology, so they're sitting in a folder on my computer waiting to either be deleted or reworked, but the ones in this book are the ones that I was proudest of, the ones I think are worthiest to fall under your eyes.

As of writing this, I only have one book out, but I've been a writer my entire life, writing stories for my friends and families and always working to craft them as best as I could. That being said, this anthology is the hardest writing task I have ever taken on.

Some days I didn't think I would be able to come up with enough stories, that I had tapped the well of creativity dry. Some days I wanted to quit, when every keystroke felt heavier than the last, when I almost shelved this project for another time or scrapped it altogether.

But then, some days the words would fly onto the pages. The ideas would write themselves, and I was just along for the ride. Some days I found a nugget of gold at the bottom of a sea of shit. That's why this anthology is called *Dark Treasures*, because the eight stories that comprise it are immeasurably valuable to me. I learned and grew so much in putting this collection together, and these stories will forever hold a special place in my heart.

I hope that when you read them, you share the same sentiments as me. I hope you value them as much as I do, because at the end of the day, that's all that matters.

So let's get on with the stories, shall we? I've explained where the *treasures* part of the title comes from; now I'll let the stories explain where the *dark* part comes in.

NO LAUGHING MATTER

The curtains closed, and the spotlight shut off. BoBo picked up the bowling pins scattered around the stage in partial darkness. They were the props he used for his final act, in which he would juggle ten pins and then his assistant would "mess up" and throw one more at him. This would cause BoBo to lose control of his act, and he'd let the pins strike him on top of his head until he "fainted."

They always laughed. But they laughed at him, not with him. That's what made it sting, that despite that he brought them joy, they didn't respect him.

With all of the pins gathered in the sack slung over his shoulder, BoBo exited the stage.

Up next would be the Magnificent Lazlo.

*

In the corridor, his assistant, a little man named Devin, was waiting for him. He was still wearing the monkey suit he wore on stage, except for the monkey's head, which was propped underneath his armpit.

"Good show, boss," Devin said.

BoBo walked past him and said, "Yeah, yeah, thanks."

He continued on until he was in his dressing room and sat down on the plastic chair some of the backstage crew had been nice enough to set up for him.

BoBo picked up the bottle of rum on the floor next to the chair and opened it. He took one big gulp. Then four more of equal size. The alcohol burned his mouth and it burned on the way down, but that was good, because it helped to drown out the voice in his mind that told him he wasn't good enough to be Lazlo's equal.

*

Lazlo sat in his changing room, waiting for the crowd to shuffle back into their seats and anticipate his arrival. His opening act, some sort of comedy routine, was mostly treated as an intermission before he came on stage. The performer would be lucky if more than seventy-five percent of the crowd was there while his (or her?) act was going on.

Plus, it gave the makeup girls some extra time to tidy his outfit up. One of them knocked on the door and poked her head full of pink hair through.

Lazlo looked up from his phone when it opened.

"Hey Mr. Salazar," she tiptoed into the room and held up the lint roller in her hand, "Just came to give your outfit the final touches."

Lazlo nodded.

She asked him if he was ready and he gave her a short answer. He didn't like interacting with the costume & makeup girls, they were always nervous around him, and he felt like he was trying to pick them up no matter how professional he kept it. He was also 54 years old, and didn't want to be one of those old perverts who hit on girls young enough to be his daughter.

The makeup girl worked the roller on his cape.

Lazlo returned to his Twitter newsfeed, and couldn't help but smirk as he scrolled through tweets with the hashtags "#WHO?dini #Lazlo".

They called him a once in a lifetime magician. Though most of the people "in the know" knew how his tricks were done, none of them could deny that Lazlo took tricks of the old and added his own pizazz to them with his performances.

A touch of magnificence, if you will.

An incoming text message came into his phone from his dearest Rosalina. She was also a magician, and though not as famous as he was, she had her own loyal fan base. And when she and Lazlo announced their relationship six months ago, her popularity exploded in its own right. Now she was able to take her shows on the road, and was currently performing on the West Coast.

The text message read:

Knock it out of the park, tonight. Love you.

He smiled and texted her back a similar message. The truth was, though he loved her, this time away wasn't all bad for him. It gave him time to get back to reading the sci-fi novels he had in his neglected backlog.

Last night in his hotel he devoured *Jurassic Park*, and tonight he planned on rereading *The Hitchhiker's Guide to the Galaxy*.

That was, if he didn't get blackout drunk as he had been doing all week. Because his alone time nowadays wasn't exactly alone time, his old pal had come to visit him while Rosalina was touring away. His old pal's name was Alcoholism.

The young girl finished up running the lint roller over his accessories, and then said goodbye and good luck to him and headed for the door. As soon as the door clicked behind her, Lazlo swung around in the chair and put his phone on the bureau where his hat was.

He opened one of the drawers and took out a flask filled with Wild Turkey.

Drinking, he tried to convince himself that he'd quit when Rosalina returned from California. He knew that wasn't likely, that Alcoholism was a friend that always overstayed his welcome, but it was good enough for the moment.

"Ahhhh," he said, slamming the flask on the bureau.

He got up, feeling the alcohol burn at the pit of his stomach like dynamite had gone off in there. Which meant it was show time.

He put his top hat on and left the room. Walking through the corridors toward the stage the walls were already beginning to spin.

*

Devin came back from watching the first fifteen minutes of Lazlo's act, smoking a cigar, and sat in the chair across from BoBo.

He was still drinking straight from a bottle of rum.

"Lazlo's been fucking up lately," Devin said.

"Oh yeah?" BoBo replied, not taking his eyes off of the cockroach that sat in the corner of the room gnawing on a piece of discarded chocolate.

His rooms were always the dirtiest and smallest, while the Magnificent Lazlo had his own personal bathroom. Shit, this room may have been a janitor's closet that they threw some furniture into when they heard Lazlo was bringing BoBo with him. There was a collection of mops and buckets in the back of the room that supported this theory.

"Yeah, he opened up with the floating woman trick and he didn't bring the hoop through smoothly," Devin said.

The trick of the floating woman act was to bring a hoop through the woman's body so that the audience can see that there indeed were no "invisible strings" keeping her afloat. However, what the audience couldn't see was the elaborate cut out on the side of the table that the woman laid on to rise "into the air." The magician stood behind the table and his job was to bring the hoop through the track and then pop it out the other end, but since the track was hidden from the audience, what they saw was the illusion that the magician simply moved the hoop through the woman's body.

The blunder that Devin spoke of was that when Lazlo passed the hoop through the track, he hit the sides of it and so the audience saw something give it resistance as it "passed through" the woman. Of course, most of the people in the audience didn't know how the trick was done, and so probably chalked it up to Lazlo's hand slipping on the hoop or something to that effect, but still.

"I think he's been drinking again," Devin continued, taking a drag of his cigar.

BoBo took a drink. "Yeah, well, that would make both of us."

"Something eating at you, boss?"

BoBo put the bottle on the ground and looked at his assistant. He didn't know how to tell him that something had been eating at him ever since Lazlo became a national sensation five years ago.

Why him? Because he was tall, broad-shouldered, handsome, and a damn good performer?

So what? BoBo was all of that... except tall, or broad-shouldered, or handsome.

Okay, so I'm only a good performer, but still.

He'd been performing and entertaining people long before Lazlo knew the phrase "abracadabra."

"Can I tell you a deep secret, Devin?" BoBo said.

The cryptic tone made Devin's spine go rigid, and he sat up straight. His eyes danced left and right, as if expecting someone to pop out from behind the closet door and surprise them.

"Um, yeah, sure," he responded.

"I want to kill him. I want tonight to be the final act he ever performs."

Devin gulped and scanned BoBo's face for any hints at him kidding around. "J-Jeez boss…"

"This is no laughing matter to me, Devin my boy." BoBo got out of the chair and crossed the room to where Devin sat. He clapped the little man on the shoulder. "You see, me and you, we've paid our dividends to the entertainment world."

"Lance," Devin called him by his real name out of fear, "have you been doing more than drinking tonight?"

"Don't call me that, you short fuck," BoBo growled back. "Call me that again and I'll fucking kill you."

BoBo wasn't sure where the rage was coming from; from Devin calling him by his real name or if it was pent-up anger or both. Suddenly, he wanted to hurt someone.

Devin gulped, and then got out of the chair and moved away from BoBo. He balled his fists, ready to fight him off if need be. He'd never seen BoBo like this before, not even with women that shot him down when he was going through one of his (many) dry spells.

"You're either with me or against me, you hear?"

Devin put his hands up, palms out. BoBo was a foot taller than him, and although not particularly imposing to normal-sized people, to Devin he may as well have been a giant. "Calm down La—BoBo, calm down, man. It's not me you're angry—"

Bobo slugged him across the face, sending one of his teeth flying out of his mouth. It bounced off the wall, leaving a blotch of blood on it before rattling to the floor.

The little man knew he was in trouble, and tried to dart toward the door, but BoBo grabbed him by the collar of his shirt, so he turned and ran the other way. The change in momentum helped him to break free from BoBo's grip, and he jumped up on the dresser in the corner of the room.

BoBo hopped over to where the bottle of rum was and smashed it against the ground, turning it into a killing weapon. The smell of alcohol seeped into the air.

Then he darted after Devin, but the little man was ready and waiting for him and kicked him on the side of the head.

The small shin cracked against his head and split him open, making BoBo see stars for a few seconds. Devin took this opportunity and jumped up on BoBo like a chimp, and bit him on the cheek.

BoBo screamed, grabbed the man by the throat and powered him off, throwing him against the wall, but Devin didn't go without taking a chunk of his face with him.

The throw sent Devin slamming against the mirror hanging over the dresser, and it smashed to pieces. The impact sent the wind from his lungs flying out, and his vision blurred, but he kept his eyes on BoBo, who was reeling back in pain.

Without taking his eyes from the clown, he grabbed a shard of the mirror and launched out at him.

BoBo saw the attack coming, and was still holding the broken bottle, so he slashed at the little man heading toward him. The glass cut him across the throat and killed him in mid-air. The arm that Devin had prepared to cut BoBo flopped to the side as his life was taken from him and his body hit the floor.

BoBo fell back on his ass and kicked himself away.

He stared at Devin's lifeless body. His hand was still curled where he had held the discarded piece of mirror that he was trying to end BoBo's life with. A pool of thick red blood was gathering underneath his head and seeping down toward BoBo, reaching out for his big shoes like fingers.

BoBo heard cackling, and he turned to see who it was. There was no one else in the room.

It took him another second to realize it, but it was him that was laughing. He put his hand on his mouth to stifle the laughter.

No laughing matter.

His hand fell away, and he laughed harder.

*

The performance was awful, he botched several of the magic tricks, but either way he got a standing ovation, as he usually did. His assistant, Brody, who wore a green suit that would have looked gaudy on anyone besides him, winked at him several times during the performance to reassure him that he was still the Magnificent Lazlo. But as he went through the corridor back to his locker room he couldn't help but shake the feeling that eventually these bad performances would catch up to him.

He returned to his dressing room and plopped down into the chair, throwing his hat into a corner of the room without a care. His phone sat atop the dresser, and its screen was lit up with an alert of a text message from Rosalina.

Reaching into the drawer with the flask, he opened it up:

Hope your show went well, sweetheart!

He smiled and took a drink from the flask. The liquor worked its magic the moment it touched his tongue and made him feel better about the shitty performance he had minutes ago.

There was a knock at his door, except when the door opened this time it was a dark, shaved head that poked through and not a head full of pink hair.

"Hey Magic, you mind if I get out of here? I gotta pick up my kids from their mom's," his personal bodyguard, Daryl, asked.

Lazlo looked up from his phone and gave him a thumbs-up. There were almost two of him, which would have been a good thing for this world.

Daryl was a big black man, 6'6" and close to three-hundred pounds, would have been an NFL linebacker if not for the knee injury he suffered early on in his college football career, but had a heart made of bonbons. He looked scary, and sometimes that's all a bodyguard needed to do, look the part. His role was as much an illusion as the tricks Lazlo played on stage.

"Have a good night, Daryl," Lazlo said.

"See ya tomorrow," he said, then his head went behind the door. A few seconds later it popped back in, "You're performing at the Lion's Head tomorrow, right?"

"That's right," Lazlo replied.

"Alright, alright, see ya tomorrow," he said, and then left again.

Lazlo opened up the contacts on his cell phone and dialed Brody. Brody was in the room right down the hall, but Lazlo liked talking on the phone when he was drunk. He enjoyed the game of anticipation between when the phone rang and when the person would or wouldn't pick up.

Brody picked up on the third ring. There was some sort of trippy, psychedelic music playing on in the background. "Hello?"

"Brode, are you busy?"

"I was just getting ready to leave the theater, why?" Brody asked.

"Wondering if you'd like to celebrate our show tonight with some drinks." He shook the flask, and the liquid only sloshed a little. "I'm afraid I'm running a little dry."

"Thought you stopped drinking?" There was an edge to the question, almost accusatory.

"I'll make an exception for tonight," Lazlo said, and then reconsidered his lie. "You know, I botched up a lot tonight, and I need something to take my mind off of it, you know?"

Brody nodded. "Uh huh, uh huh."

"So, what do you say?"

"I mean, yeah, but——"

"Great," Lazlo said, "so go down to the bar and bring whatever you want. I don't care what as long as it'll get us nice and drunk and sting on the way down. Put it on my tab."

"Alright, alright Boss," Brody said, with a small chuckle at the end. "Give me about fifteen."

*

He had torn off the clown shirt, bowtie and frills and all, because blood had sprinkled on it when he slashed Devin's throat open. BoBo stood in front of the mirror. His hair was parted to one side, almost jet-black in color from the dampness of the sweat his scalp was producing. He had washed off most of his makeup, but had done a shitty job and there were still blotches of it here and there on his face.

"Pitiful loser by day," he scowled, "Lazlo's shadow by night."

Killing Devin had been bittersweet, like a cup of black coffee. Mostly bitter, though, because Devin had been his only friend. The sweet part of it was the power he felt coursing through him—it was almost electrical in its charge.

He smiled at his reflection. He was thin, but had a gut like a snake in the middle of digesting a rat. The nipples at the end of his flabby chest were hard. He reviled himself day in and day out, but this was the card he was dealt in the looks department.

Not like it mattered, most people had no idea what the hell he looked like without the BoBo makeup. Lance Fache—as his birth certificate called him, was a shadow to his clown persona, and his clown persona was a shadow to Lazlo.

In some ways, Lance didn't even exist. Which was fine by him, because now a new person had been born. When he killed Devin, something had awoken inside of this paunch, pale body. Some might call it a murderer, but he was thinking it was something more ethereal. A demon, perhaps.

"It felt good to kill him, didn't it?" His reflection grinned back at him. "Oh yes, yes it did."

There was a razor sitting on the edge of the sink, probably left behind by someone who had been doing coke. BoBo grabbed it and stared down at it. He could drive this across Lazlo's throat, and end him. End everything.

No more sitting in his changing room, drinking shitty liquor to drown out the envy that stung him every time the crowd cheered for one of Lazlo's stupid magic tricks. No more being second fiddle to someone less deserving than him.

BoBo put his finger on the edge of the razor and swiped it across to feel how sharp the edge was. He began to bleed, and it dripped into the sink.

That felt good, as well.

*

Daryl closed up the locker room where his bag had been and walked down the empty corridors, whistling some free-form tune to himself. Most of the lights in the backstage were shut off, and the only other noise was coming from a radio attached to a janitor's trash bin at the end of the hallway. Other than that, there were no signs of anyone being around. The back of the theater was closed for the night.

Suddenly a door down the hallway, maybe twelve yards away, opened up, and a figure stepped out of the room. There were shadows thrown across the person, obscuring who it was.

"Yo," Daryl said, hoping to surprise the person as much as he had been surprised. He thought everyone except Lazlo and his entourage would be gone by now.

BoBo stood in the cover of the shadows, watching the big man stride toward him. He seemed cool as a cucumber, while BoBo himself was pickled. He never realized just how big Lazlo's personal bodyguard was until the moment before he had to kill him.

He'd have to be quick, and his timing would have to be spot on, because if he fucked this up this guy was going to kill him—kill him accidently or on purpose, it didn't matter, but he was going to kill him if BoBo didn't kill him first.

All he had was this stupid razor. He suddenly wished he would have grabbed the broken bottle.

"Yo, what's up?" Daryl said again, continuing toward him.

It was go-time, he couldn't waste any more time without looking suspicious. BoBo stepped out of the shadows.

Daryl stopped, not because he felt threatened, but out of concern. He thought it was a poor homeless guy that had wandered into the theater somehow.

"Hi, can I help you?" Daryl asked.

He doesn't even know who the fuck I am without the makeup. BoBo thought, his anger flaring up even more.

"You lost?" Daryl continued.

BoBo nodded and then reached into his pocket for the razor. "I've been lost, my friend. I've been lost underneath Lazlo's shadow for too damn long now."

BoBo saw the man's arm twitch as if to reach for the gun at his hip, and then stop and relax. This was his moment to seize.

He jumped at him, pulling the razor from his pocket and aimed to slash his throat. Daryl stepped back, quick enough to redirect the attack, but not quick enough to get out of harm's way, the blade sliced across his face, sliced one of his eyeballs open, sliced the bridge of his nose, and cut the eyelid off of his second eye.

Daryl had reached for his pistol the moment he saw the razor in the BoBo's hand, but then the pain made him throw it away and reach out for his face instead. The gun clattered to the floor and fired off once.

Daryl stepped backward, grabbing at his eyeball and trying to keep it from falling out of the socket, while blood ran through his fingers and down his hand in a waterfall of thick crimson.

BoBo slashed his throat open with the razor. The slice in the middle of his throat spurted blood out like a broken sprinkler and then the man's lifeless body toppled over.

BoBo leaned against the wall, his heart pounding in his chest. He felt the warmth of the bodyguard's blood dripping down his chest. But more importantly, he felt the power of killing charging through him.

Then he remembered that the pistol had gone off, which meant anyone still in the theater would be alerted of the happenings by now. He would have to find another time to revel in the thrill of the kill, because in a matter of moments he'd be found out. He'd have to act quickly if he was going to kill Lazlo.

*

Lazlo heard the gunshot, and at first thought it was just something falling in another room and his drunkenness was exaggerating it to his senses, but then the brooding feeling that something had gone bad crept over him and he jumped out of his chair.

He went to another drawer in the dresser, opposite of where he had kept his flask, and took out his six-inch butterfly knife. It had a white handle and was bejeweled. He thought of it as more of a novelty item rather than an actual weapon, but he carried it around with him just in case of instances like whatever was happening out there at the moment.

The world spun around him, spun and tilted like he was on a ship caught in the middle of an impossible whirlpool with a rising tide underneath it. But he couldn't think about that, something was going on, and somehow he knew (magic, perhaps?) that his life was in danger.

He pushed through the dressing room door and went out into the darkened corridor. The back of the theater had a different feel to it now, no longer were there staff members going in and out of doors and no longer were the murmurs of conversation echoing off the walls, now there was nothing but silence and shadows all around him.

"Hey! What's going on out there!" He yelled out into the expanse of the hallway, then instantly regretted it when there was no reply.

From behind the shadows and down the hall he heard footsteps approaching, then he saw the ambiguous outline of a shadow. The person approaching him was small in comparison to Lazlo, but his stride was all confidence.

When the person stepped out of the shadows and was underneath the pale fluorescent bulb, he knew why; the crazy man wielded a gun. He pointed it at Lazlo, and to his surprise, Lazlo didn't feel any fear at all.

All he felt was pity for this poor fool.

"Okay, sir, put the gun down." Lazlo said.

The man took another two steps, and Lazlo saw he was wearing yellow shoes that were at least two sizes too big. He traced the shoes up the leg and saw he was wearing bright red pants with white polka dots on them.

The pants. The shoes. The nose. The stupid smile. It was all vaguely familiar, but there was a mental curtain keeping him from making the connection, from the alcohol, probably.

"I don't think you're in the position to be making demands, Magnificent." BoBo took two more steps, which put him within arm's length of the magician.

He could see in his eyes that Lazlo wasn't sure who he was, and he couldn't help but feel a pang of pain. He thought that on some level Lazlo had respect for him because he'd been his opening act for two years now, but no, it seemed BoBo was in the right all along. Lazlo had no idea who he was.

Which meant he had no respect for him, and he was going to pay for that.

"You have no idea who I am," BoBo said. His smile faded and turned into a frown.

Lazlo nodded. "I do, actually."

BoBo thrust the gun forward. "Oh yeah? Then who am I? Huh? Tell me."

"You're, you're..." He was almost there.

Damn this alcohol.

It had gotten him into trouble many times (and gotten him out of it, as well) but this time it may be the end of his life. Not because he got behind the wheel, but because of some lunatic in a clown outfit—

Right then and there it hit him. *Ta-da.*

"It's you, BoBo," Lazlo said, and smirked despite the situation.

BoBo took a step back, as if Lazlo had smacked him across the face. "So, you do know who I am?"

"Of course," Lazlo said, and spread his arms out, a gesture he did after a successful trick on the stage. "How could I forget my partner?"

"Oh no, oh no. I'm not falling for this shit," BoBo gripped the gun tighter. "I know what you're trying to do."

Oh, you have no idea what I'm trying to do. Lazlo thought.

If he could buy himself just enough time, Brody might be coming back from the bar in time to stop this crazy man from harming him.

"BoBo, I don't know what's gotten into you, but you don't need to do this. You're better than this."

BoBo scowled, and then wiped the sweat off his forehead with his free arm. "Stop it!"

"The man who innovated the pie-in-the-face trick is reducing himself to wielding a gun, and for what? More money? We can write up a new contract, BoBo."

Lazlo hoped that the pie-in-the-face trick was a part of the clown's act, if not, he had just given away that he was lying.

Luckily, it was, and it was one of BoBo's favorite acts to perform because in his mind he *did* innovate it by having Devin shoot the pie at his face from a mini-catapult.

"Y-you're just trying to buy yourself time," BoBo hissed. "Well, guess what? There's no one here to save you. It's just you and me."

BoBo tilted his head back to gesture behind his shoulder. "Your bodyguard is lying a bloody mess over there. And you'll be lying next to him soon. You can't pull a disappearing act in the real world, buck-o."

Lazlo put his arms down and hung his head down. "What did I do to you, BoBo? Why are you doing this?"

"Why? *Why?* Because I've lived in your shadow all these years, and what do I get from it? Nothing. No fans, just people who recognize me as the sideshow for you. I've been entertaining people for over twenty years, and I don't have a single fucking fan."

The anger bottled up inside of him took over, and BoBo pulled the trigger. The shot was wild and missed entirely, going at least three feet over Lazlo's head and hitting the wall behind him.

Lazlo ducked out of instinct, and then quickly realized no harm had been done. He expected another shot, but it didn't come. He looked up from his crouch and saw BoBo was sitting down on the ground, the gun lying at his side.

"You see Lazlo, and I'm sure you get this, but those on the outside probably don't. But us entertainers, we're all one in the same. Stand-ups, magicians, actors, writers, all of us, we all want to be recognized for our talents.

Some of us make it in this world, through different means. But you, you've made it like only a few of us ever have. But you take it for granted, you drink too much, you fuck up performances, you show up late for shows."

BoBo picked the gun up again and aimed it right at his face this time. "And I'm here to put a stop to it... this is just desserts."

Lazlo made his eyes cry, the first trick he ever learned when he was a child to get his mother to give him one more cookie when he was still in diapers. "Please, BoBo, don't do this. Please."

"Tears of a wolf," BoBo said, getting up.

He pulled his foot back, and with one long shoe, he kicked Lazlo in the face. Lazlo grabbed his bleeding nose and fell flat on his stomach.

"Any last words, Magnificent Lazlo?" BoBo said, and aimed the gun at his back.

Lazlo couldn't respond, because he was too busy howling in pain from his broken nose.

*

The first gunshot he heard made him want to turn and run, but the second one made him think better of it. Lazlo was still back there in his changing room, waiting for him to show up with the liquor from the bar, which meant he might be in trouble.

Lazlo, the man who took him under his wing when he was just a doorman at the Red Horse theater. Lazlo, the man who started up a charity in his own name for his mother's heart transplant a year ago when he needed help paying her hospital bills.

He couldn't just turn and run and leave him behind after all he'd done for him.

Brody grabbed a piece of rebar lying next to a wall, a few feet away from a room that was being remodeled. Wishing he had something better than this skinny metal bar, he sprinted down the hallway toward the source of the noise.

When he got to the action, he saw a doughy man hunched over. He couldn't see what he was staring down at, but he had a feeling whatever was going on was bad. Brody ran past Daryl, and glanced over for a second to see him covered in blood, but didn't let the sight of it slow him down any.

He loaded up the rebar in his arms as he approached the man in the middle of the hallway and let it swing through the air when he got within hitting distance. The metal slammed into the back of the man's head with a thud, and he fell forward from the blow.

Brody didn't let up, and hit him across the back. The man screamed in agony as the metal bar smacked against his spine. He hit him again, this time on the head, and continued to hit him until his skull cracked and blood poured out like lava.

Eventually, the man's body went still.

*

As the metal bar was hitting BoBo in the back of his head repeatedly he could only think one thing; Lazlo was actually magic, and had somehow disappeared from the floor to behind him and was killing him now, instead of the other way around.

He would have laughed, if not for his brain being half shut off by the time the thought passed through his mind.

Then he heard a gunshot, and BoBo would hear nothing ever again. Nobody would ever laugh at him, or make him feel lesser again.

*

Lazlo sat against the wall, sweat dripping down his face and his heart beating against his chest so fast he was sure he was about to have a heart attack. Brody sat next to him, staring at the body of the clown—or whatever this guy was supposed to be. There was a gunshot wound in his back where Lazlo had used Daryl's pistol to finish him off.

"You saved my fucking ass," Lazlo said, feeling silly that he was stating the obvious, but he was so grateful that he couldn't help but say it.

Brody put his hand on his shoulder and said, "Who the hell is that guy?"

"The clown that used to open up for me," Lazlo said, staring at the lifeless body in polka dot pants.

"Jeez," Brody said, and then after a long pause asked, "was he funny?"

Lazlo shrugged. "Not like it matters, no one is ever going to laugh at him now."

FROM DOWN BELOW

Underneath Trexlerville, Pennsylvania, a mutation was occurring, out of sight from the very people who would become the creature's victims.

Chemicals from a coal factory were being dumped into the sewer system, giving life to a new lifeform. The company responsible for it, Titan LLC, didn't bat an eye at dumping the chemicals, it cost them less and was more favorable to their bottom dollar.

If caught, however, they'd be fined heavily. As such, they were meticulous in that not happening.

If only they had known the terror they were creating down below, perhaps then they would have stopped.

*

Just twenty days ago, it had been living off the sewer water and rodents that ran through the tunnels, but it had been smaller then. Now its head was the size of a beach ball, and its six legs—though muscular—were weakened and seemed to drag the heavy shell on its back with more and more difficulty each passing day.

Its stomach grumbled, and the creature knew it needed to do something or it would starve. Then the rats would be eating it, instead.

There had to be a way out of this maze. Its mind turned to the slants of light that came in from the top of the walls. If it could somehow get up there, it would find a new world, perhaps one with more resources than it was finding down here.

The creature dragged its body to one of the walls. The edge of its shell clanged against the concrete with each plod forward.

Clang. Clang.

It never tried this before, perhaps because it had never been desperate enough. The creature put its front feet on the wall, and then it stepped, just as if it were stepping on the ground. Its next two feet followed and latched onto the wall, and then it continued its climb up, heading toward the surface, to a new world where it hoped to find meatier food.

The movement was new, but the creature only took a few moments to realize it was the same as walking on the ground, and then it began to move quicker. The bottom of its shell bounced off the wall.

It reached the grate a few seconds after that and peered through the bars. It saw two feet, similar to its own, in leather sandals. The toenails were painted purple. There was another set of feet, but these were bigger and wider. It followed the feet up to the legs that they were attached to, and saw they were hairy. Not like the rodents it found down below, but more hair than the creature itself had on its own body, which was none at all.

It wondered if the four feet belonged to the same creature, and if they did, was this creature similar to itself?

It didn't matter. Either way, the creature was going to kill and eat whatever it was.

Using the claws on the front of its body, the creature grabbed the iron grate and tossed it to the side, careful to put it down so as to not alert its prey.

The feet on the surface began to move away from it, and the creature's black eyes flashed.

The hunt was on.

*

Holding hands, they strolled down Arbury Park. It was Fourth of July Weekend, so the trails were void of any activity. Most people in Trexlerville were down at the Saratoga River (known as just "the Saratoga" to all of the locals, mind you) or Glenn's Lake swimming and barbecuing, but not Joy and Ned.

They were shy, reserved people, which was what had brought them together in the first place, so they invited the quietness of the park. It was just them, in love and strolling down the paved lanes, listening to the chattering of the birds and the scurrying of the chipmunks.

Joy was careful to not call him "The One" because her last boyfriend had burned her badly, left her for a thinner blond girl he met at his new job, and she didn't want to experience that awful pain again.

But she also couldn't ignore the feelings, the shivers she got every time they held hands or kissed. That part was undeniable, and she knew she would have said "yes" if he asked her to marry him right this second.

She didn't realize it until he turned to look at her that she had been staring at him this whole time. He grinned, and said, "Watcha lookin' at? Something good, I hope."

"Maybe the best-looking thing in the park," she replied, and smiled back at him.

He didn't take the compliment the way she had been hoping he would. In fact, he didn't take it any which way, because his eyes suddenly went pallid. His mouth gaped open, and a stream of blood flowed down his lip and dripped off his chin.

Ned's body slumped forward, but didn't fall. Joy looked down at her boyfriend's stomach and saw a giant lobster claw sticking out from the middle of it, covered in his guts and blood and holding up his lifeless body.

The claw retracted, and Ned's carcass hit the ground (The One, no more).

She screamed and jumped back, but her legs turned to rubber and she lost her balance. She hit the ground ass first.

Joy stared at the creature, at first thinking it was a giant hermit crab. Then she saw its shell was flat, more like a tortoise's, and she realized this thing was like nothing she had ever seen.

The creature swiveled on the balls of its feet and crawled after her at an unexpected speed.

Its shell clambered behind it, *clang-clang.*

Joy kicked at the creature, but it deflected the attack with one claw and reached out to pinch her ankle with the other one. She felt the serration of the claw break through her skin and grind against her bone, and screamed at the top of her lungs.

The creature pulled her closer, then using its free claw, snipped her head off with a single pinch. Her head went flying into the air and then rolled across the grass until it slammed into a tree, leaving a trail of blood in its wake.

The creature returned to Ned's body and began slurping up his intestines like spaghetti dinner.

*

Doug Marzullo stopped his cruiser a few yards from the couple's messy remains. He unhooked the radio from the dashboard and called back to the park ranger's office.

"Hey Ray, I got something here," he said, almost not believing it.

"What?" Ray said back.

"I'm not sure, looks like…" Doug looked out of the windshield to make sure the scene was still there, that it hadn't magically changed before his eyes, "looks like murder."

"Ah, what the hell," Ray said, and Doug could almost hear his partner taking his feet off the desk. This was supposed to be a slow week for them, so much for that. "I'll dial Trexlerville and then meet you over there."

"Alright," Doug said, "I'm going to get a closer look."

He hooked the radio back on the dashboard and then got out of the car. Almost tiptoeing and almost shitting his pants, he made his way to the two bodies.

It was worse than he imagined. The woman's head—and he could only tell what remained was a woman because of the tattered skirt—had been decapitated by something sharp. Her limbs had chew marks on them, but whatever had eaten her had decided the good stuff was in the center, because the torso was torn open.

The second body lay only a few feet away, and this one was just as bad except for still having a head attached. The man's face was twisted in the pained agony he had experienced in the final moments of his life. His entrails hung out from the middle of his stomach like a jumble of computer cables.

Doug's initial thought that this was murder was dispelled. Whatever had killed these two people had done it to eat them. They had been hunted down and slain like prey.

He heard some bushes rustle to his left, and he turned to face them, gun drawn and readied, but it was just a chipmunk that froze when it saw Doug looking in its direction.

Doug took in a deep breath, and hoped Ray and the township police would show up soon.

*

The creature returned down to its home, to the darkest and dampest part of the sewer labyrinth there was, and rested on its belly. It was exhausted from the trip above and from the thrill of hunting down the hairless prey.

Everything up there had been too much for its senses. The green surroundings had been vibrant, and unlike the green mold that grew on the walls down here, it hurt its eyes.

The most unsettling part of the experience had been the blue and white dome that seemed to expand into forever. Something that seemed so large if it fell it would destroy everything below it, and not just that, it also moved. The white splotches on the dome moved as if they had a life of their own.

But the creature knew it would return to the surface, because the hairless prey had satiated its hunger. They tasted better than the rodents and were easier to catch. Their blood was sweet and its mind craved for a taste of it despite that its stomach was full.

Just thinking about it made the creature want to go back. But instead, it closed its eyes, and with a full belly for the first time in weeks, it went to sleep.

*

The next morning the creature climbed the same wall to the same grate where it had attacked the couple in Arbury Park. It didn't climb out into the daylight yet; there was no activity besides a few rodents with fluffy tails that scurried by. They were similar to the rodents below, and the creature made a note that it could replace them if the ones in the sewers ever ran out.

After forty minutes of watching, to no avail, the creature began to climb back down. Its stomach cramped halfway down the wall and the need to defecate ushered it faster. On the mouse and rat diet, it only needed to go two or three times a week, but the hairless prey meal seemed to be moving right through its bowels.

Once back in the sewers, the creature jumped into the water and excreted. Relieved of its duty, it climbed back onto the walkway. Using its four upper eyes, the creature searched for the next grate up above, while its two lower eyes focused on what was in front.

There were more grates all over the sewer system, and it suspected it would find more success the more ground of the area up above it could cover.

So it lumbered through the sewers, its heavy shell clanging against the concrete with each plod forward.

*

Clang, clang, clang.

Kevin had his ear pressed up against the grate on his street. The metallic sound coming from down below was mesmerizing for some reason, maybe because he had lived on this street for 8 years and never heard the sound until last week when it was raining and he was playing water-rescue-mission with his army men in the gutter.

He told Mommy about it, but she barely glanced at him from her sewing machine where she was fixing Daddy's pants. So he told Daddy, he put his newspaper down and said "Ooh yeah? It's probably just loose metal that got down there somehow," then picked up his paper and took a puff of his pipe. Neither of them had seemed very interested.

But if they heard the sound for themselves...

Kevin kept listening to the metallic sound coming from somewhere underneath him.

Clang.

Clang.

Clang.

He didn't think Daddy was right. It wasn't just metal going through the sewers. He was 8 years old, but not dumb. Daddy had just been uninterested because he hadn't given it a chance to play its sweet melody for his ear, to mesmerize him the way it mesmerized Kevin.

Clang.

Clang.

Clang.

"Kev! Lunch is ready!" It was Mommy yelling out for him.

Kevin felt his stomach grumble, but at the same time, he wanted to keep listening to the music, too. He could eat roast beef sandwiches any time of the day and week, but he didn't know how long the sounds would last, so he kept crouched below the curb, hoping Mommy wouldn't see him.

She called out one more time, and he waited a few seconds before popping his head up to see the screen door shutting behind Mommy. She knew he always came home around lunch time; he was a good boy about that, and she wasn't overly concerned with not seeing where he was because he often hung out by the creek over the hill.

And he would return. As soon as the beat of the metal sound calmed, he'd gather up his army men and head back inside to eat lunch and watch *Teenage Mutant Ninja Turtles*.

The metal tune got to the point where it was always loudest, and then it would fade out until Kevin couldn't hear it anymore. He wondered if he followed the sound to the next grate on Maple Ave, on the other side of the hill, if he'd be able to hear it, but he would never do that.

He saw this grate, this spot, as his own personal concert from whatever was down below, and didn't want to ruin the illusion by finding out that the tune played throughout Trexlerville. It was similar to when they went downtown to the parade; no one followed their favorite part of the parade, even though you could. No, it was much better to pick a spot and watch the performers pass your spot, and pretend like the show began and ended where you were.

Kevin waited for the sound to begin to die down, but it didn't, this time the tune took a different turn. It grew louder.

CLANG.

CLANG.

CLANG.

The sound was different than what he was used to. There were fewer echoes, and more abrasion to it, like something that was once sharp but now dulled was being dragged between each metal clang.

Kevin kept his head near the grate, but turned to look into it. Nothing but darkness and slimy stuff all the way in the back.

"Hello?" He said into the darkness.

But the only response was the metal clanging, louder now, and getting louder with every second.

Maybe Daddy's right. Maybe it is just something that broked in the sewers.

He was ready to get up, now that the magic tune wasn't so much a tune, but the sound of metal bouncing against concrete, the show was over. The tricks had been revealed, and the wizard behind the curtain was underwhelming.

But there was one more act, an act Kevin didn't expect. An act no one could have expected, really.

The metal clanged one last time, right underneath Kevin. Although he was ready to go home, he felt as stiff as a stone as he looked at the darkness beyond the metal grate.

"Hello?" He repeated.

This time, the response was a claw coming out from between the bars. A claw like the crayfish he and Evan Liston sometimes caught down by the creek, only bigger. Much bigger, big enough to—

The claw grabbed at him, and Kevin jumped backward, but not quick enough. It pinched him by the front of his shirt, making the Donald Duck graphic go cross-eyed, and pulled him forward, slamming his shoulder against the curb.

Kevin screamed, screamed as loud as he could. He kicked at the ground and punched at the claw, but the blows hurt his knuckles more than it could've damaged the claws, because they were hard as a lobster.

Another claw popped out from the darkness, and it worked the grate loose, then moved it to the side. Since Kevin and the first claw were being separated by the metal bars, the second claw moved around the displaced grate and pinched him by the waist.

He felt the serrated claws rip through his flesh, and blood seep out of the wound and soak his clothes. Kevin screamed in pain, screamed in desperation, screamed in regret.

The claw around his waist pinched him harder, then the second claw punched through his stomach. A flash of hot pain spread through Kevin's whole body as the claw ripped through his back.

His young life flashed before his eyes, and then he went still, never to eat another roast beef sandwich again.

*

The creature carried the two parts of Kevin Barnes' torso through the sewers, one piece in each claw. This hairless was smaller than the two hairless it had caught the day before, and the creature decided to try to bring the food with it instead of leaving it on the surface.

By taking the limbs off the body, and then cutting the torso into two crude halves, the creature was able to squeeze its leftovers through the grate and bring it down. It had eaten most of the insides, but there was plenty of flesh on the bones for later.

The creature retreated to its nest in the corner of the sewage system and threw the two pieces of torso in the opposite corner of where it slept. The body parts hit the walls with a meaty thud and sprinkled blood on them.

Another full belly, another successful day of hunting. If catching the hairless prey on the surface kept being this easy, the creature might never have to leave the sewers. It could just surface when it needed more food, then return below.

With these thoughts on its mind, it closed its eyes and slept.

*

Officer Hernandez found himself tossing and turning in his bed, not able to get a wink of sleep.

He kept seeing the crime scene in his mind; the boy's limbs lying about the gutter, the cut on them was crude, like something jagged had been used to remove them. An old hacksaw, perhaps.

But it didn't add up. Something about the whole thing rubbed Diego the wrong way, and kept his mind from resting. They lived in a small town where everyone knew everyone and their business. If someone had gone looney and decided to murder a child in the middle of the street in the middle of a summer day, they would've been outed by now.

And the possibility of it being someone out of town made even less sense. Trexlerville wasn't exactly "on the way" to anywhere, which means the person would have gone out of their way just to come into town to murder a child.

Sure, there were people who were batshit crazy, but even they had to value their time somewhat.

He couldn't take it anymore. It was bugging him too much. He jumped out of bed, put on a pair of jeans and a shirt, grabbed his keys and his handgun, and headed out the door.

*

Randy Campbell looked up from the report they were preparing to release to the local news when he heard his office door open. Officer Hernandez came in with slightly disheveled hair and wearing street clothes.

Randy looked at the clock hanging on his wall and then back at his officer. "Hernandez? What the hell are you doing here, son?"

Diego sat down in the chair in front of the sheriff's desk. "I couldn't sleep."

The sheriff put his pen down and leaned back in his chair, inviting Diego to say more.

"I've been thinking about the boy who was killed today."

"You and I both," Randy replied.

"More specifically, I've been thinking…" the words got stuck behind his mouth.

The sheriff was sort of a father figure to him, he had coached the football team back when Diego was in high school, and had helped him get on the squad a few years after he graduated, but his thoughts sounded crazy even in his head.

"Go ahead, I'm listening," the sheriff encouraged.

Diego coughed. "I've been thinking that maybe there's something in the sewers."

"Like in that Stephen King story about the clown?"

Diego felt his cheeks grow hot. "Not quite like that."

"Then what? You think a murderer is hiding in the sewers?"

Diego shrugged. "Perhaps, sir. I think it's worth—"

The sheriff banged his knuckles against the report in front of him. "Look, as bad as this might sound, it's our job to keep the peace and order in town, and part of that is sometimes letting things blow over."

"What do you mean?" Diego looked at the sheets of paper the sheriff had his hand over.

He could only make out some of the words but he knew that it was the official statement regarding the two deaths in Trexlerville they were putting out for the local news outlets tomorrow morning.

"What I'm saying, Diego, is that I'm not about to send the police department on some escapade to find a monster from your childhood in the sewers." The sheriff took in a deep breath, then went on, "What most likely happened was some crazy guy driving through our town decided to go on a killing spree.

It's happened in our town before, thirty years ago before you were even born, son. It'll probably happen again."

"So that's the story you're running with?" Diego said. The heat on his face had turned from embarrassment to heat of anger.

"Yes," he tapped the report again, "that's what we're going with. Look, son, don't confuse the badge on your uniform with a mask and cape. We can't nail every bad guy storming through our world. They're unpredictable, that's why we call them crazies."

"What about the couple found in Arbury Park? You don't think that was connected to Kevin's death?"

Campbell sat up in his chair. "It probably is, but there's not much of a lead here. If it keeps happening, then we'll have stronger reason to look into it, but for now, we'll leave it at that."

A silence fell between them. Then the sheriff said, "Is there anything else I can help you with?"

Diego got out of the chair, and shook his head. "No, sir. I think that's it."

"I suggest you go home, have a drink or two, and try to forget about this. Trust me, I'm worrying enough for the both of us as it is."

Worried about saving face. Diego wanted to throw out at him, but instead just nodded and said: "Understood, sir."

He told the sheriff to have a good night, then turned and left the office. He had felt defeated in the midst of that conversation, but now that he was away from it he felt a surge of invigoration go through him.

There was something lurking in the sewers, and if the sheriff wasn't going to do anything about it, then he'd have to take matters into his own hands.

*

Diego parked his car in front of a house with pink shutters that didn't really match the rest of the façade, across the street from where a square of yellow caution tape barred people from entering the crime scene. He didn't know why, but it felt better to keep his car at this distance— in case he needed to get away, perhaps.

He got out of the car and went over to the crime scene. Slipping under the tape, he saw that the clean-up team had done a good job of getting the stains of blood out of the concrete, but how it had looked earlier in the day was still burned in his mind.

He could see the dark spot where the boy's blood had pooled, he could still see the exact spot where each of his thin limbs had lain. Even worse, he could still see Mrs. Barnes clutching one of Kevin's army men and sobbing while he and his partner asked her husband questions about their son.

He coughed to clear the feeling of his throat closing up on him, then put these thoughts to the side and let the cop side of his mind take over.

Diego kneeled down in front of the gutter. There was a thick cover of tape between him and the opening, but he had a hunch that that wouldn't stop whatever had killed Kevin Barnes from getting him, too.

Seeing the scene again reinforced his thoughts that there was something in the sewers.

Something with sharp claws or teeth, judging from how the limbs had been separated from the rest of the body. Also, where *was* the rest of the body?

He had an idea that taking a tour of the sewage system would bring him to it.

Officer Hernandez put his ear against the tape. He didn't hear anything coming from below except the rush of flushing water and maybe rats skittering through the tunnels.

No metallic tune like Kevin had talked about to his parents.

A lightbulb went off in his head. If whatever was down there had come after Kevin, then maybe he could lure it to him, lure it out of the gutter and kill it right here on the spot.

He kept packages of beef jerky in his car as a snack for when he worked late nights. They were usually a post-workout snack too, but tonight they'd serve another purpose.

Diego raced back across the street to his car and popped open the trunk. He grabbed a bag of jerky from his gym bag and then returned to the gutter.

He took two pieces, fat and thick, and placed them in front of the yellow tape. Then he took out his Swiss Army knife and cut a hole into the layer of tape. One quick slice and it ripped open big enough for him to slip some pieces of jerky through.

He sat back on his haunches, drew his gun out, and waited.

Down the street, the last light shining on Applegrove Lane winked out.

*

While Diego waited for the creature to take the bait, down below it continued to sleep.

It would continue to sleep until his eyelids grew so heavy he couldn't keep them open anymore, and then he'd turn back to his car, drive home, and fall into bed like a rock.

*

Diego was up at 6am, ready to go. His alarm didn't go off because it was his day off, but his internal clock woke him. He took care of what he needed to do: let the dog out, brushed his teeth, changed out of his pajamas into street clothes, and grabbed his gun plus some ammo.

In the kitchen, he opened up a cupboard above his sink and stared at a box of Raisin Bran for almost a full minute before deciding to skip on breakfast.

Considering where he was going, this may have been for the best.

He headed out the front door, grabbing the keys to his cruiser on the way out.

*

The access to the sewage system was in the woods behind Valley Lane, which was more like a sparse collection of trees where children often played during long summer days. There was even a small treehouse on one of the big oaks.

It was too early for any children to be playing, and they wouldn't be playing outside much today after what happened to Kevin Barnes yesterday, anyway.

Diego found the big, vault-like door to the sewer access. It was down a gulley and hidden behind moss and brush. There wasn't so much brush that you needed to bushwhack to get to it, but there was enough there to keep it hidden from plain sight, to keep the neighborhood kids from finding it.

He grabbed the wheel on the door and gave it a spin. It gave him some resistance and creaked, as if something had built up on the rotation device it worked on, as if no one had used it in weeks— maybe months. He turned it again, and this time it moved easier. The next few spins were smoother, and the door opened on its own.

The smell of sewage wafted out from the opening and rushed into his nostrils. He wasn't known for having a weak stomach, but even he couldn't resist putting his shirt up on his nose to make the smell a little less offensive.

He unhooked the flashlight from his belt and turned it on. Then he pulled the door open. The smell of the sewers seemed to be jumping out at him now, and the beam of his flashlight did little to cut through the darkness.

Alright Diego, let's do this, he said, trying to pump himself up, but knowing damn well the smell was only going to get worse down there.

The darkness would, too.

*

It didn't take him very long to find the trail of blood that would lead him to the creature's nest. The sewer system was a maze of its own, but Officer Hernandez had a keen sense of geography and had grown up in Trexlerville, so the map in his head of where he was relative to the streets above was easy to navigate.

The darkness wasn't as bad as he had anticipated, either. He still had to use his flashlight to see in front of him, but he wasn't in pitch blackness. The light coming in from the grates above also helped some.

He found himself underneath the grate on Applegrove Lane where Kevin had been killed. On the street above, they had bleached out the blood, but down here the boys blood still remained on the walls. It was hard and crusty, but still had the shape of when it had been gooey and dripping.

Diego shone his light to see how far up the blood ran. While he did that, he kept his ears perked to any activity in the sewers; water sloshing too quickly, footsteps trying to sneak up on him... metal clanging.

The blood indeed ran up the wall and to the grate on Applegrove Lane, so there was no mistaking whose blood it was.

He shone his light on the walkway in front of him, and sure enough, there was a trail of blood. It streaked across the ground like someone had been dragging a giant paintbrush behind them. He knew if he followed this, he'd find Kevin Barnes' torn body... and also whatever had done it to him.

For a second he thought of turning back to the cruiser and radioing the station for back up, but then the sheriff's words rang through his mind.

I'm not about to send the police department on some escapade to find a monster from your childhood in the sewers...If it keeps happening, then we'll have stronger reason to look into it, but for now, we'll leave it at that.

He had embarrassed himself enough already, and besides, if he did catch the murderer down here the sheriff would have no other option other than to recognize that he had been right in pursuing this.

With that in mind, Diego drew his gun and stepped into the sewer, ready to take on whatever he might find.

*

Click-clack. Click-clack.

The creature awoke to the alien sound bouncing off the walls of the sewer.

It was something stepping toward it. Something had found its hideout and was coming after it.

Its heart beating fast in its chest, the creature rose up on all of its legs, and its six eyes peeled back.

Click-clack. Click-clack.

It looked in the corner where its food was stashed and saw it was still there. At least there was that.

The invader's steps grew louder. Whatever it was that was coming after it was coming from the left tunnel. The creature jumped into the water, submerging itself.

It didn't know what to expect, but it knew whatever the thing was, it was being drawn here by the food. And the creature wasn't going to let its food be taken away without a fight.

*

Diego stopped when the beam found the torn body in the corner, across the tunnel on the other side of the water. What remained of Kevin Barnes, of the sweet boy from 1324 Applegrove Lane, barely resembled a human. It was more a mound of flesh and blood bound with torn cloth than a child.

He moved the light away, his stomach able to handle the sight of it even less than the smell of the sewage.

He flicked his wrist left and right, scanning the rest of the tunnel with the flashlight, and saw nothing else of interest. He shone the light into the water. It was still, and too dark to see if anything was hiding down below.

Diego touched the extra clips attached to his belt, grateful to have had the foresight to bring them with him, and aimed at the water.

He pulled the trigger.

The moment the bullet broke through the surface of the water, the creature lunged out from underneath, its claws heading straight for him.

Diego stepped back and pulled the trigger again. The bullet went through one of the creature's feet, but that didn't stop it from pressing forward. Once it got to the walkway, it began to climb up toward him.

Diego jumped back and shot at the damn thing again, but before he could realize he was shooting a shell, the bullet bounced off the top of the creature's body, and it was moving in on him again.

Its claw reached out at his shin, and Diego hopped back just in time. Moving backward through the tunnel he had come in from as quickly as he could, he took aim at one of its claws and fired. The bullet tore through the protective exoskeleton and exploded the flesh underneath.

The creature's mandibles opened, and it screamed. Despite the fact that one of its feet was hanging on by a thread of skin, and bled profusely, Diego thought this was the first real damage he had done to this abomination.

He continued stepping backward, aimed, and fired again. This time he missed, by mere inches, but that was enough time for the creature to have recovered.

It turned and ran the other way, leaving a trail of green-brown blood behind it.

"Oh, no you don't, *maldito*." Now it was his turn to move forward.

He chased it, but the thing was quicker than he thought it'd be, and it hopped back into the water just as Diego fired another shot at it. Again, he missed.

Seconds later, the creature surfaced out from the other side and climbed up the walkway. Diego aimed the barrel of the gun, but from his angle, it would be too difficult to hit anything except its shell. It would be easier to walk around the water and meet it on the other side of the tunnel.

He sprinted toward the back of the tunnel, and crossed the walkway over the water to the other side.

The creature scurried to the body, to its food, to exactly where Diego thought it would go. It thought he was trying to take its food.

The creature stopped for a moment to grab the two pieces of the body. Diego shot at it, hitting two of its legs, and the bullets tore them right off of its body. The creature threw its claws in the air, the damaged one sprinkling blood all over the sewer walls, and let out another scream of anguish. The body parts fell from its grip, and the creature tried to scoop them back up, but by that time Diego was at its side.

He kicked it, as hard as he could, and sent the creature crashing against the wall. When the shell and the concrete met, there was a ringing sound akin to a church bell going off. The creature landed on its back, and just like a tortoise flipped upside down, it couldn't get back to its feet.

Diego aimed his gun at the center of the creature's stomach, where it looked to be soft and fleshy, and unloaded his clip into the creature.

When the deed was done, the creature's hole-ridden underbelly stopped rising or falling. Its entire body was drenched in its ugly blood.

Diego Hernandez stepped back until he felt a wall behind him, leaned against it, and then sat down on his ass, panting hard and dripping in sweat.

He looked over at the remains of Kevin Barnes—only for a second, and then he had to look away. He put his head between his knees and prayed for the child's soul.

Halfway through Our Father, he stopped at the sound of the water sloshing.

Diego picked up his flashlight by his feet, which he had dropped at some point, and looked over at the creature: still on its back, still oozing blood, still dead.

He aimed the flashlight to the water and saw the surface bubbling. Then the head of another creature surfaced, followed by claws.

Diego jumped up to his feet and reached for another clip to load into the handgun.

He shined the light back on the water with the gun aimed, and froze again when his flashlight revealed that all of the water as far as he could see was bubbling.

More heads poked out, ten of them, maybe, but it may as well have been a thousand. All of the creatures began to climb the side of the walkway and headed toward him. Their claws pinching the air, their six black eyes focused on him.

"Fuck!" Diego screamed.

But down here, no one could hear him.

BIG BAD

In a little village known as Cavenall lived an old woman. Every week she would bake a pie from a new recipe she was experimenting with, and while it sat and cooled, she would sit on the porch of her pink house and write to her granddaughter, who lived across the country in a town known as Pumpernich, on the westernmost side.

Each letter opened with the details on the pie, then was filled with updates on the neighborhood's children, about how big and handsome the boys were growing and how pretty and polite the little girls were. Before sealing the envelope, the old woman would put in a handful of honey roasted peanuts or a peppermint candy in the envelope.

Because Red was the oldest of four girls and was her father's only help to tend the farm, she did not visit her grandmother very often. About once a month or so. Most of their communication was through these letters, and in the stationery, their bond was built and maintained.

But one day, things in the town of Cavenall went bad, and the letters to Red stopped.

*

The first week went by with no letter.
That's fine. Maybe Grandma is busy, she thought.
Then the second week, there was no mail once again. Now she and her father began to worry.

The third week, she waited for the mailman on the steps in front of her home. He came up the incline, the ass he rode on huffing and puffing from overwork. Red stood up as the carriage stopped in front of her and he reached into his satchel for their mail.

"Thank you," she said, taking the stack of envelopes. She noted grimly that there wasn't a colorful one in the mix.

The mailman pulled his cap in salute, and then urged the poor donkey down the hill and on to the next house.

Red rifled through the envelopes. A letter from the town tax collector, a letter from the blacksmith downtown, and then some advertisements from some of the local shops, but nothing from grandma.

*

"The blade, as well," Red's father said, handing her a sheathed short sword. "You don't know what dangers lay ahead."

There was trouble where Grandma lived, of that much they were sure. What that trouble was, Red planned on finding out. Father wanted to go, but she volunteered. There was a lot to be done around the farm. It had been a good season for their crops, and Father had to prepare for the big festival at the end of the quarter of the year.

She was well-equipped with weapons. A bow and a quiver of arrows that she used when they went elk hunting, and a short blade. But both she and her father were holding on to the hope that Grandma had just come down with influenza and wasn't much in the mood to write.

"Better to have it and not need it," she said, quoting him as she hooked the blade on the side of her belt.

Her father winked at her, then put his hand on her shoulder and kissed the top of her head. "Don't go and get yourself into trouble now, Red."

Red grinned, and before either of them said anything, they heard the hooves bouncing down the road on the beaten path, alerting them that the carriage that would take her to see Grandma was near.

Up above the hill overlooking their small home, the clouds were thick and dark. A heavy rain was likely to commence soon, and Red put the hood of her robe up in preparation.

The carriage came over the hill, and the mare pulling the carriage was the converse of the mailman's donkey—beautiful and strong.

Red turned to her father and gave him a hug. "I'll be safe, I promise."

"You better be," he said, and kissed her on the cheek. She reciprocated.

The carriage stopped in front of them, and they separated.

"Good evening, folks," the chauffeur said, preparing to get out of the carriage to help Red onto it.

Red waved her hand to him. "No need, sir."

She took a pouch of gold from inside her robe and handed it to him, which brought a smile underneath the chauffeur's curly mustache. He took it, emptied the coins into a bigger sack lying by his feet, and then folded the pouch into his shirt.

"We leave when you are ready, milady."

Red checked that the blade was at her side, slung her bow across her shoulders, and then picked up her bag of belongings and climbed into the carriage.

"See you soon, sweetheart," her father said.

Red waved good-bye to him, then told the chauffeur she was ready to go. He obliged and tugged on the reins, the mare pulled the carriage through town and into the woods.

*

They couldn't afford the carriage fare from Pumpernich all the way to Cavenall, so she was always dropped off fifteen miles from Cavenall and walked the rest of the way to Grandma's house through the woods.

Red climbed out of the carriage and thanked the chauffeur. The chauffeur told her to have a good day, and then turned around to double back.

The rain on this side of the country wasn't coming down yet, but the clouds suggested there would be a downpour. Thankfully, the carriage had dropped her off in front of the Lakepond Restaurant, a cozy establishment in the middle of the woods that was in no particular town, but had a regular flow of patrons from the surrounding villages to keep it afloat.

Red was one of these regulars, but today when she went into the restaurant the patrons all avoided eye contact with her, making her feel unwelcomed.

Even Thomas, the bartender, just nodded to her out of politeness then turned back to filling patrons' beer mugs.

All of the usual folks were there:

Sammy the Glassblower, who couldn't have weighed more than a hundred and ten pounds even on payday when his pantaloons would be overstuffed with gold coins.

His wife Bertha, a woman whose bosom shook every time she laughed.

Billy, the cross-eyed boy who carried around an impressive bug collection in a jar.

And then there was Winston, a man with a reputation as tough as the scar running across his face suggested he would have.

Red walked past them to a table in the corner. Only Billy said hello, and the rest kept to themselves as if they didn't see her.

*

She ate by herself, and even Hilda, one of the restaurant owner's daughters, treated her indifferently when she brought the sausage platter to her.

Either they all decided they hated her from her last visit for some reason, *or they know what happened to Grandma*, she thought.

Winston had glanced over at her multiple times when he thought she wasn't looking, but Red had been quick enough to meet his gaze a few times. After he finished off his fourth beer since Red had come in, he pushed the barstool back and got up.

He marched over to her table and sat across from Red.

"Hello, Winston," she said, cutting into her sausage.

"Hello, Red," Winston said, and drummed his knuckles on the table. His eyes kept darting over to the bow and arrow on her back. "You lookin' real equipped there."

There was an edge to the words that Red didn't like. "Does a lady wielding weapons make you nervous, Winston?"

Winston laughed, and Red was hit with a blast of the smell of alcohol. "Do you even know how to use that thing?"

The roles of women and men were well-defined in their country. Women were supposed to stay at home and tend the house: bake bread, churn butter, care after the children. Men tended the farm and hunted, but Red's father broke that tradition since he had no son and his wife had passed away giving birth to their last daughter.

"My Father taught me how to use it. He was in the army." She waved her fork at him. "And considering he has no scars, I assume he's better at using weapons than you."

Winston crossed his arms and leaned back. Instead of getting angry, he smirked and changed the course of the conversation. "I assume word has traveled all the way to Pumpernich?"

The lack of a retort took Red by surprise. Winston wasn't known to be calm and cool. "Word? Word of what? What are you talking about?"

The glee on Winston's face disappeared, and his eyes grew big. "You mean...you don't know?"

Red put the fork down. It clinked against the side of the plate, making the gesture more dramatic than she intended it to be. "Don't know what?"

He shook his head, and more to himself than to her he said, "I thought that's why you came equipped."

"Spit it out already, Winston," she urged.

Winston gathered himself and came back to the conversation. "You really don't know about the monster of Cavenall?"

"Monster? What monster?"

Winston looked at her bow again. "I really thought that's why you had that thing with you, that you intended to slay the beast."

Red clenched her fists. "What beast? Just tell me, dammit, quit skirting around it."

Winston would have never let anyone talk to him in this manner, but he understood the distress the girl was under. He had just broken the news to her that her grandmother had likely been eaten by a monster.

"The stories are that it's a manbeast. Half-wolf, half-human. Others think it's some form of demon," Winston told her.

Red felt her heart expand in her chest, and her mouth went as dry as cork. She took a drink from her water. "Who is telling these stories?"

"Those who managed to flee Cavenall and the surrounding area. Word is, the beast had been terrorizing the surrounding towns before showing up in Cavenall."

Red shook her head. "Why would Grandma not mention this?"

Winston shrugged. "Perhaps she didn't want to scare you. People were dismissing these stories in the same manner they dismiss other scary tales. Until it was too late."

That seemed like a well-enough explanation for her, after all, Grandma's letters were cheerful and a rumor of a monster in town wouldn't have been in alignment with the tone her letters carried.

But still... perhaps she would have mentioned *something*. Maybe even just in her letter to Red's father.

"The beast just showed up one day and destroyed the town?" Red asked.

Winston nodded.

She leaned back, her fists clenched underneath the table. "And no one tried to stop it?"

"The way it's been told to me is that the beast did it in one huff and puff of its breath, and destroyed everything in Cavenall."

"Ridiculous," Red muttered.

"Ridiculous? Perhaps," Winston said, and leaned across the table closer to her. "But it's true, Red, I've seen it with my own two eyes."

"The beast?"

"No, the destruction," he was speaking in a low tone now, although the other patrons in the restaurant already knew all of this. Red thought it was the alcohol making him more dramatic.

"I came back from Cavenall two nights ago. Everything is in ruins."

"That means I have a beast to hunt," Red said.

"You're mad." Winston's eyes bulged.

"Perhaps, but I'm mad in more than one sense," she said, getting out of her chair.

The other patrons turned in their chairs to look when she did this. They had all been listening to the conversation, but now they were captivated.

"I've come prepared for danger," she said, and took out an arrow and held it in front of her face in case he forgot she had weapons on her. She twirled it between her thumb and index finger.

"The beast is said to have big claws."

"Is that so?" she said, still staring at the arrow.

"Yes, all the better to slash your innards out, Red."

"Let me guess, do these tales also tell of it having big teeth?" She grinned, but it wasn't a happy grin. It was a grin that came out of anger.

Winston's face flushed. It was unbecoming of him to feel embarrassed, but here was a young girl willing to hunt after the beast when he himself was too frightened to do so after seeing what it had done to Cavenall.

"All the better to eat me with?" Red prodded on.

Winston gritted his teeth. "That robe you're wearing won't do you any good to protect you, Red."

She put the arrow back in its quiver and looked at the robe. "Yes, I suppose you're right."

Winston shook his head. "I don't think you understand what you're getting yourself into."

Red stared at him, and Winston stared back at her. The bar collectively held their breaths in anticipation.

Winston rose out of his chair, his gaze still locked with hers. "You've no experience slaying beasts, and this beast slayed an entire village in less than a day."

"And you have experience in slaying beasts?" Red asked.

"More than you do, and I wouldn't mess with this one even if I was paid handsomely for it."

"I'm taking this beast down for free," Red said, and started for the door. "My motivation is more valuable than a couple of sacks of gold."

She marched through the restaurant, saying goodbye to the others and dropping a handful of gold coins on the bar to pay for her meal. Then she stormed through the front door, slamming it against the wall in the process.

Climbing down the steps she was back on the road in the woods.

Behind her, Winston called, "It was nice to know you, Red."

Then he added, "Good luck."

*

It began to rain as Red made her way down the windy road in the woods toward Cavenall, so she put her hood up. She couldn't help but admit that Winston was right; the red robe would make her an easy target for any beasties in the woods. Not just the big bad one she was looking to catch (if it didn't catch her first), but any other beasts that might be lurking beyond the trees. Suddenly, the sausage she had chowed on wasn't settling in her stomach very well.

She grabbed the hilt of her sword, prepared to unsheathe it the moment any danger was present. Despite the bravado she had displayed in front of Winston, the darker the sky grew and the closer she came to where the beast would be, the more nervous she grew.

Something her father had said when she was twelve kept echoing through her mind like a mantra.

Facing one's fears instead of turning away from them is what separates the brave and the bold from the spineless and cowardly.

They were out deep in the woods when he had said that, elk hunting, and he noticed how nervous she was despite her trying to hide it. Back then, her only experience in the wilderness was when she and her friends played hide-and-go-seek in the first twenty or so yards in the woods.

He had drawn the bow, and said that quote seconds before the arrow whizzed through the air and through the heart of an elk. After that, he taught her how to gut it out, and then, on a fallen tree, he butchered it into sizable chunks for cooking.

The memories shattered when she saw the wooden sign pointing toward Cavenall. Up ahead the road inclined, and then she'd be at grandma's village. Or rather, what remained of her grandmother's village.

Red took the blade out and followed the road. Ready for whatever may come.

Beast, man, wolf, a little of each; it didn't make a difference. It had eaten her grandmother, and revenge was all she had on her mind.

*

In her mind, Red could still see and hear the town as it once stood. She could hear the children laughing as they ran down the cobblestone paths, zigging and zagging to avoid crashing into the adults walking to the courthouse to pay their taxes or to the post office to send out a letter.

The piles of splintered lumber and rubble were the remnants of the establishments she had known so well. Bethany Childe's bakery, where she and Grandma went to get strudels on many summer nights after dinner, was a pile of colorful metal and lumber. Across the street, Old Al's Butcher shop was nothing more than splintered wood strewn about, covered in blood. The two-story courthouse in the back of town had toppled in on itself, and the sign hanging on the second-floor awning that read COURTHOUSE hung crookedly.

There was something else in the air, too. Not quite a smell—but a feeling, a feeling that something dreadful had swept through Cavenall. If it weren't for her knowledge of the beast, Red would have guessed a heavy storm had hit it.

In one huff and puff.

Grandma's house was in the northern part of the village. Red walked down the hill and through the town until she was at the fountain that decorated the middle of the village. It was dry, except where the shadows were that the sun hadn't touched.

She looked up at the statue of the man in the center of the fountain, he had his hair brushed back, a beard and glasses, and wore a long coat.

There was a fishing rod in his hand and a Labrador with its tongue sticking out at his side. The dog held his snout up in the air, proud and obedient in perpetuity. No one knew who this statue was supposed to depict or who had built it; the townsfolk thought it was older than the village itself.

It was something that the fountain was the only thing intact. A good sign, perhaps.

Red continued through the town, looking around at the disarrayed village, still not quite believing that a single beast could have done this.

As she got closer to Grandma's house, she noticed that the houses weren't as destroyed as they had been at the southern entrance of the village. Their windows were broken, as if someone or something had been thrown through them. The shards of glass were sprinkled about the houses. Some of their walls and roofs were littered with holes, and she could hear the pitter-patter of the rain falling inside them and bouncing off the floor or upturned furniture.

They were in bad shape, but nothing that a little time and effort couldn't have fixed up. It seemed the beast's attacks were concentrated at the entrance of the village, and not back here where Grandma's house was. It gave her hope—but only a sliver.

She walked past the shoe repair shop, the wooden sign that hung on the awning now lay on the ground in multiple pieces, then she made the turn to where Grandma's house stood. It was mostly intact, and the pink painted bricks stood out more than usual considering the destruction that surrounded it.

Red climbed the steps, they creaked underneath her feet. Something she hadn't noticed before, something that seemed only to matter at this moment, as well, because she could hear something inside of the house. She stopped by the front window, and listened.

She heard scratching coming from past the foyer, past the kitchen, from the room that Grandma used to sew her bonnets and fix Red's pantaloons.

Red moved from the window to the door. She tried to swallow, but her throat was suddenly coated with something thick and grainy. Fear, perhaps.

She turned the knob and opened the door. The lock had been busted at some point (*someone trying to save Grandma*, Red thought), and the door swung right open. Before Red stepped into the foyer, she stopped.

The hardwood floor was covered in a trail of blood, slimed through the hall and into the room where the scratching was coming from. The blood looked bright and fresh, a recent killing of whatever monster was haunting Cavenall.

Sword in hand, Red pressed on, careful to avoid stepping in the blood.

The scratching got louder as she approached the sewing room. A metallic clang startled her and froze her for a second as something heavy fell from a high point in the room. Then, whatever was in the house with her was scratching at the fallen object.

Red made the turn that put her in the entrance of the sewing room and stopped once again when she saw the beast. It had its back to her, and half of its body was inside of a chest. In the upturned room, with the sewing machine lying to one side and broken in pieces, spool and thread thrown about every which way, Red barely recognized the chest, even though she had seen it many times. It was where Grandma kept the clothing that needed to be fixed.

The beast stopped chewing on the arm of the child that had been hiding inside of it when it heard the floorboards creaking underneath Red's steps. Its ears perked up, and it swiveled to face her.

The rumors Winston had heard were partly true; the beast was indeed a wolf. However, the part of it being half-man seemed to be false, because this creature was not half-man, but all beast, despite that it stood on its hind legs and used its front legs like arms.

There was a bonnet strewn over its head, covering one ear. The wolf reached up and tossed it off, and then opened its mouth, which was smeared with red from the child's blood—like lipstick.

Red anticipated a war cry, or a howl, but instead a voice came out.

"What are you supposed to be? Some sort of hero?" The wolf's face twisted into a smirk.

All at once, Red realized how silly she looked. A red robe, a sword that she had never used except to cut apples in mid-air to show off to her little sisters, and facing off with a monster that destroyed an entire village.

She cleared her throat to make sure it didn't squeak when she talked. "Maybe not a hero, but I'm here to kill you."

The wolf tilted its head back and laughed. The laugh was animalistic somehow, like a tiny bark was echoing behind every sound. "You'll suffer the same fate as this town, little red. You'll be just a snack."

Red looked at the beast's claws. They were gigantic, sharp, and thick. No way did she want to get up close with the wolf. In a motion faster than even she thought she was capable of, Red sheathed the blade and stepped back while at the same time drawing her bow.

She nocked an arrow and took aim. The wolf had stood there for a second, confused by her movement, but now it was coming after her.

Red took a deep breath to center herself, just how her father had taught her, and then let the arrow go.

The arrow whistled through the air and stabbed the wolf's neck. Again caught by surprise, the wolf stopped in its tracks and howled in anger and pain.

Another opportunity, another few seconds to seize. Red nocked another arrow, pulled the bow back, and let it fly. This time the wolf was ready for it, swiped it away with its paw, and then ran after her.

Red stepped backwards, and her back hit the wall. She had to run either left or right. Left would take her out the back of the house and right would take her through the house.

She opted to run through the house and started sprinting away just as the wolf's claw slashed where she had been standing a fraction of a second ago. The claws ripped through the wall, pulling dust and wood into the air.

The wolf continued to chase after her.

At the end of the hall, Red stopped and pivoted on her heels. She shot another arrow at the wolf. He tried to claw it away like the last one, but was too slow this time, and the arrow went through the beast's paw. Blood sprayed from the wound, but the attack didn't slow him any.

She considered shooting another arrow, but there wasn't enough time, so she sprinted out the front door and stamped down the stairs.

The downpour continued, and its drumming drowned out all other noise. Red had no idea how close the wolf was to her now, but she continued to run as fast as she could.

This was all a mistake. I should have turned back when Winston tried to convince me to, she scolded herself, then pushed the thoughts away and sped her pace up.

Up ahead, the fountain was a few yards away. She craned her neck, taking her chances, and saw the wolf was just coming out of the house. The arrow still stuck out from the top of his paw like a naked flagpole.

She stopped, nocked another arrow, and waited until the wolf was out from underneath the awning of the house before taking aim.

This time her target was his legs, to try to slow him down.

She let the arrow go, and it arched through the air toward the wolf's thigh, but the wolf moved faster, and he sidestepped it. Then continued his charge.

Red shot another arrow, the distance between them closing with every second, she didn't care where this one struck as long as it struck the wolf. But it didn't, because by now the wolf was privy to the speed of the shots, and again sidestepped it.

The wolf reached out for her, the claws flashing even underneath the gray sky. Red jumped backward, but it wasn't enough space. She felt the nails rip through her chest, and felt the hot release of blood seep through the gash.

The blow knocked her backward, and she tripped on her own feet, but she kept the bow clutched to her chest and tumbled through the grass. Her momentum kicked up clumps of dirt, until she slammed into the fountain.

She felt a hot pulsing on the top of her head where the impact had occurred, and knew it'd turn into a nasty knot tomorrow.

If there was a tomorrow.

The wolf pounced, this time with his mouth open, ready to bite a chunk of her flesh off. Red rolled aside, and the wolf had to throw his arms out to stop himself from crashing into the fountain mouth first.

Red took this moment to draw her blade out of its sheath, get up, and stab the creature. The point of the blade went through the forest of dark fur until it penetrated through the skin. She drove it in as deep as it would go and felt an organ pop. Its liver, or maybe a kidney.

Whatever it was, it was enough to make the wolf drop to its knees. Red pulled the blade out of the beast and then stabbed it again.

This time she drove the blade through its chest and punctured its heart. The wolf snarled, and growled, and reached out with its claws, but when they got to her they were too weak to do any harm. The arms fell away, and the beast fell backward, defeated but not yet dead.

Red got up and stood over its dying body.

She reached down and twisted the handle of the sword, ripping the wolf's chest open even worse. The wolf let out one final growl, and then was dead.

For Grandma.

Red sat on the rim of the fountain, suddenly light-headed, suddenly dizzy. Black curtains appeared in her peripheral vision, and they teased that they would close, and then would open, and then close again. She blinked, but that did nothing.

And now she was aware of more than just the trickles of blood dripping down her body; she was aware of the pain where the wolf had ripped her open. There were four claw marks: one was just above her breasts, another was centimeters below her throat, and then two more sandwiched in between. They burned and stung at the same time. She had been able to keep the wolf from killing her with that blow, but not from injuring her badly.

She tried to get up, but the blood loss was turning her legs into cooked noodles, and she was forced to sit back down or topple over, so she sat down.

"No, no, no," she muttered, trying to keep her consciousness.

If she didn't get help soon, she was sure to die.

Those were her last thoughts before the curtains closed.

*

When she woke up, she was in a strange room. The shadow of a single flame danced on the wooden ceiling above her. The bed she was in was big and soft—maybe a little too soft for comfort, and seemed to be swallowing her.

She moved the cover off her chest and looked down. She was wearing a blue shirt, and underneath the shirt she saw she was bandaged up. Red sat up on the chair, against a pillow that was also too soft, and scanned the room.

It was bare except for the bed she was on and a wooden table next to it. Even the walls were bare, just raw wood without a single decoration to be found.

On the table was a glass of water with a lemon in it, a melting candle, and a loaf of bread. She was about to pick up the glass of water when there was a knock on the door. It opened, and a lady with a face that was a perfect circle and thick brown hair poked her head through the opening.

"Oh good, you're awake." The door opened more, and the thick woman came through, carrying another glass of water with a lemon in it. "Got you some more water."

The lady set the glass down and then sat on the end of the bed.

"I'm sorry," Red said, her voice dry, "but where am I?"

The lady patted her on the thigh. Her hand was warm and gentle. "Winston found you in Cavenall and brought you back to our home."

Red's mind took a second to unscramble. "Winston?"

"Mhm, he says he knows ya from the Lakepond Restaurant. You're a semi-regular there or something?"

Red couldn't help but smile. "Yeah, that's right. He went all the way to Cavenall to find me?"

She nodded. "Yeppers. He's out getting some wood for the stove, but he should be back soon, then he'll fill you in on the details."

Red took the glass from the table and sipped some water. "Yeah, okay. Thank you."

"Say, I gotta ask, what made a young gal like you go out there?"

"My Grandma," Red said, and thought of all of the good times she had with her, and how the wolf had eaten her.

"Oh." The woman's eyes dropped to her feet, and there was a slight pause before she said, "I'm quite sorry to hear that."

Red nodded.

The woman got up and headed for the door. She opened it, and then said, "Name's Tabitha, by the way."

"I'm Red, nice to meet you, Tabitha," she replied.

"Pretty name. Well, you're welcome to stay until you feel you're good and ready to go back home. I'll tell my husband to check in on you later on, but get some rest, kiddo. You still look tired."

"Yes, I think I will. Thank you." Red said.

Tabitha disappeared through the door and let it click behind her. Red didn't know what time it was, the room had no windows, but she knew she still wanted to sleep. She blew out the candle and got under the covers.

She slept, dreaming of fairytales.

FLOWER GIRL

Despite what people on the internet who defend me say, I'm everything the media has made me out to be. My name is Carl Sabatini, and I'm a murderer.

This is my confession and recounting of that night. I'm writing these words down to make amends with Him.

We've worked out a signal, though, so when he comes to take me into the next life—to take me to Hell—I won't even fight it. I'll go without question. I don't think I deserve any mercy, not after what I did, not after the monster I've become, but He knows better than anyone what I deserve.

The people that read about me in the morning paper over their cups of coffee, the newscasters that judge me from their high chairs in studios, yeah, He knows what I deserve better than them, too.

We all have a cross we're nailed to. The difference is, I can see mine now.

*

You've probably read the interviews by witnesses who saw me leave the party I attended that night, and they all swore up and down that I was sober and in good spirits when I left, that there was no chance of this act being caused by a drunken, blind rage.

Let me clear the record. That was a load of bunk—those people were all paid off by my lawyer. Don't ask me how he did it, I'm not sure how, but he used his pull to get the right people to say the right things about me.

The money wasn't anything crazy. After all, in some way this was coming out of my pocket, but the type of people at the party were the kind of people who live paycheck-to-paycheck, so it was a sweet deal for them.

It was only sweet for them and my lawyer during the trial, because it did nothing for the guilt that hangs over me every day, threatening to crush me with its weight.

I wish it would.

Here's the truth: I was drunk when I left that party. Really, really drunk. Before I was a murderer, I was an alcoholic. I was recovered up until that night, but the events that led to getting drunk were the straw that broke the camel's back, so to speak, and I found my old demons in cans of Coors Light once again.

The first mistake I made wasn't drinking, though. The first mistake I made that night was bringing Glenda to the party with me. Glenda wasn't exactly my girlfriend; she was more of a fuck buddy, and I would've dumped her two weeks before if it weren't for how crazy she was in bed.

But I digress.

So we show up at the party, and Glenda gets right down to business, guzzling down some spiked punch with pieces of fruit floating in it. Apples, I think. I felt like a Grade-A square, just standing there with my hands in my pockets while everyone around me was getting smashed.

I convinced myself to have just one, and one turned into several. Me and Glenda start to get all touchy-feely, so we made our way down to the basement. Except the alcohol was working against me, and I couldn't get it up, so I ended up just servicing her with my tongue and fingers until we both had enough, and then we headed back upstairs to the party.

We went our separate ways; I went into the kitchen to help myself to more booze. I figured I already fucked up when I cracked open my first beer, so I may as well fuck up all the way. Glenda went into another room, where the extra party favors were in baggies and came in the form of white powder.

While she was partaking in nose candy fun, at some point I got in the middle of an argument with some fat asshole named Kenny. We were arguing about Clinton and Trump, or some bullshit about politics. This was the height of my drunkenness so the memory is a bit fuzzy.

Either way, I found myself in a screaming match. Those around us laughed at the sight of a skinny bald guy (me) and a fatso in a sweaty polo whose face was the color of a baboon's ass screaming at one another.

This next part has been recounted to me from a source that I imagine would rather remain anonymous. While I was in the middle of this argument, Stanley, a co-worker of mine, was talking it up to Glenda in the other room. Flirting with her, being a smooth operator, trying to finish what I couldn't in the basement earlier on in the night.

The thought of it makes me angry even to this day.

They went out of the house, and my source followed them for reasons you can probably guess if you put your mind in the gutter and take into consideration that Glenda has big plastic tits.

Eventually the screaming match with Kenny ended with me blitzing through the crowd gathered around us and looking for Glenda. I was tired of drinking, tired of the loud rock music, tired of the people laughing at me. All I wanted was to leave.

I poked my fingers around the pockets of my jeans for my keys, and to my surprise, they weren't there. I figured I might've dropped them or something, so I barged through the front door. Behind me, I could still hear people laughing.

The cool November air stung my face, but it felt good. It felt better than being laughed at by thirty drunken jerkoffs I barely knew.

Tracing my footsteps back to where I parked my car, I looked in the grass and on the street for any sign of my keys. A twinkle in one of the lawns or anything like that, but I didn't find anything.

My car was in view, and I could see that someone was in it, so I approached it. Thinking I was getting robbed, I picked up a rock from someone's lawn and tiptoed over to the back window.

I found the whole shebang that would start this awful night. Stanley was in the back seat of my Prius, his head tilted back on the headrest and his face twisting in gross satisfaction. I stepped closer to the window and rapped my knuckles against the glass.

"Get the fuck out of my car," I said, as Glenda removed her head from his crotch and looked up at me.

She was so far gone that the moment didn't register for her, and she smiled when she saw me. Stanley was frozen in the seat.

The door was unlocked, so I pulled it open and repeated my command, "Get the fuck out."

Stanley slid out of the seat, yanking his boxers and pants up as he did so. For a moment when he was out of the car, we stood face-to-face, and I wanted nothing more than to slug him.

But I held it together, and instead I dropped the rock I was holding. I didn't want to make matters worse. Funny, in a cosmic way, looking back on what happened later that night.

He finished buckling his belt, then looked at me like he was going to say something, but stopped himself. Instead, he turned and went back to his house.

I turned to Glenda, who had lipstick smeared all around her lips and mascara running down her eyes, and I said the same thing to her, "You too, get the fuck out."

She got out of the car, smiled, and said, "Oh, baby, you know I didn't—"

I shoved her away, with more force than I probably intended, and this was enough to get her to shut up and comply. She reached into the car to grab her pocketbook from the passenger seat and then jetted away.

She probably assumed I'd get violent otherwise, and I probably would have. It was like the devil was raging inside of me at the time.

I looked at my backseat, and there was a stain I'd have rather not known the origins of. Disgusted, I turned away and saw my keys lying in the front passenger seat. Perfect.

I snatched them up and then settled into the driver's seat.

As a veteran of being drunk (and I have a rap sheet of hours of community service and Alcoholics Anonymous to prove it), I knew I shouldn't have been behind the wheel, I knew I shouldn't have turned that damn ignition on, but also speaking from a veteran's point of view, I also knew I didn't give a shit.

There was an entire library waiting for me on Pornhub and some leftover spaghetti from dinner the night before. All I wanted was to get home.

Maybe my lawyer could have used that as a defense. *Your honor, my client was under duress at the time. He was on an empty stomach and had blue balls.*

If only.

*

With the house hosting the shitty party, the shitty people, the shitty woman I brought to it, all in my rearview mirror, I started feeling pretty good. The Coors Light I was loaded on helped as well. I turned the radio up. It was on a hip-hop station I didn't remember tuning to, but it didn't matter. Any music would have done the job then.

I was feeling badass from telling Stanley to fuck off and for leaving Glenda abandoned. I was so giddy and joyful that I swerved in and out of lanes. Some of the time it was from my own doing, other times it wasn't.

I managed my way through the backroads of the neighborhood, bumping the curb only once or twice, but I never came close to hitting a mailbox or knocking over a fence. I was proud of that. Eventually I found my way out of the neighborhood and onto the boulevard. I headed north toward the highway, toward home.

A police car with its lights off sat in the parking lot of a convenience store, facing the boulevard. Officer Dipshit must have been stuffing his fat face or sleeping, because he somehow missed my speeding Prius as I whizzed by with only a patch of grass and a sidewalk between us.

I looked in my rearview mirror as I drove toward the onramp. Any second the car's lights would turn on and he'd be on my ass, but it never happened.

It would've been a blessing in disguise had he pulled me over, because then I'd have a DUI, and that's it. I wouldn't have a coffin in my head every waking second—sometimes every sleeping second, too, depending on the night.

Once I got on the onramp and my Prius was behind the protective barrier, I knew I was scotch-free, not just from being pulled over by Officer Dipshit, but from the rest of the night as well. Four exits down the highway, a couple of left turns, and I'd be home in my apartment and able to put this all behind me.

Of course, fate had other plans in the cards for me. *He* had other plans for me.

*

One moment I was racing down the highway, radio turned up, the next thing I knew my eyelids grew heavy, my head began to loll forward, and then I was fast asleep. No volume of KRS-One was going to help me win over the fatigue and booze I was battling against.

After that, the next thing I remember was hearing the screech of my tires. I opened my eyes to see my car headed straight into whiteness. A wall, I thought. This was the end; I was going to turn into mush on impact.

Since this is a true confession, I will add this even though you may not believe it. Seconds before the collision, I saw Him staring at me. He was formed by the reflection of my headlights on the waxed surface of the limousine, stood there like an apparition. He was staring at me with scornful eyes, eyes that said, *I died for you once Carl, but I'm not dying for you this time. This is your sin to bear, your cross to carry.*

And then the hood of my car smashed into the side of the limousine, and he was gone.

If it weren't for my seatbelt, I would have been launched through my windshield and splattered against a wall or a tree—whichever was in my path first.

If only fate would have been that merciful.

After the crash, I sat in my driver's seat. Not quite all there, but I had tears running down my cheeks. You know that sensation you get when you know you've done or said something bad, but you can't quite pinpoint what it was? Yeah, I had that sensation prickling all over me, and at the time I didn't know it, but it was the onset of the guilt I'd have to live with.

Something in my radio must have busted because as I laid my head against the steering wheel, all I could hear was the whirring of my tires still trying to move forward. I reached out, my head still on the steering wheel, and put my car in park.

Outside of my car, I heard yelling and shrieking. It was distant, and I was so out of whack that I couldn't tell where it was coming from. It could've been coming from right outside of my window, or from down the highway, or from another state. New Hampshire, maybe.

I felt the cold November air rush into my car. This time it didn't feel so nice.

*

The first responders were already there by the time I got my bearings under me and crawled out of my car. The EMTs split into two groups. One group was checking up on the family outside of their ambulance; tending to their wounds and trying to calm the mother down. Her shrieking was piercing. The other group of EMTs were setting up curtains around the scene.

A state trooper, a thin Hispanic man, was setting up flares on the side of the road. The other one, a black woman, was in charge of keeping the rubberneckers moving along. It was well past midnight when the accident occurred, 2:37 am was what I read, so there weren't many of them, but just the same she waved them to keep going.

Nothing to see, folks, just another drunk who fucked his life up.

I pushed between three photographers barricading the damage the vehicles had taken and saw that I couldn't discern where the hood of my Prius ended and where the side of the limousine started. It was all just a jumbled mess of plastic, metal, and wires soaked in blood and oil.

No one had asked who I was at this point, and no one seemed to care. Judging from the damage done to both cars, I imagined I was presumed dead, but by some grace (or disgrace) I wasn't.

On the other side of the limousine, I saw more cameras flashing, so I stumbled that way, wondering what could possibly have their attention. You'd think the scoop would have been the damaged vehicles, but something a few yards away was juicier, apparently.

Everything around me seemed to merge into colors with no definition, and I had to blink several times before my vision returned.

One of the times I blinked, I found my eyes locked on to a man in a suit that would have otherwise been sharp if not for it being torn at the legs and splattered with blood. An EMT was bandaging his arm, and my vision was well enough to see the broken bone sticking out of the middle of his forearm. It was an ugly break, like a dry tree branch that had been snapped, and dipped in blood.

He stopped answering the questions the EMTs were asking him long enough to meet my eyes, and the look haunts me even to this day.

I headed toward the other group of photographers, feeling Coors Light and bile crawl up my throat, thinking the driver's arm was the most damage I caused. It couldn't have possibly been worse; after all, I would have been the one to take the brunt of the damage, and here I was walking.

I pushed past the photographers, who by now were walking away, and saw how wrong I was. When I saw what had them so damn intrigued.

The world seemed to disappear in that moment. Nothing but me and the girl's body existed. And then, all at once, my demons jumped out in front of me.

*

This is the part of the confession where you'll grab your stone, and ready it to throw at me. And that's fine, because no matter what sins you've committed, I doubt they're worse than what I did.

As it was described to me by my lawyer, the hood of my Prius was just high enough that when the car t-boned the limousine, it hit Mandy at the right level and angle to decapitate her. Her father had been sitting on the opposite side of her, and the window was rolled down to let the smoke of his cigarette out, and when my vehicle rammed into the car, her head went flying out of the limousine.

The impact threw her head between the father and the aunt before clearing through the window. The aunt recounted in a newspaper that she thought a bat from hell was flying at her, that she had no idea what it was, until the rest of Mandy's body landed on her lap.

The mother remembered reaching out to grab her little girl, who didn't have a seatbelt at the time because God knows why, and feeling her ankle slip out from her grip as she was lunged forward from the impact.

Some of the people in the comments section of articles about this incident have tried putting the blame on the parents for not buckling her in. Some have tried to say it was the driver's fault, that if he hadn't been texting at the time (I'm not sure where this rumor originated, but it started somehow), he could've avoided the accident altogether. I think these people are just people who want to stir up shit on the internet, but either way, they're wrong.

Make no bones about it. The blame lies all at my feet for getting behind the wheel that night, whether it was from sadness or anger doesn't make much of a difference. There are no ands, ifs, or buts about whose fault it was.

This truth, that it was all my fault, didn't strike me as hard until I saw her lying in the grassy patch off the shoulder of the highway. She was belly-down and wore a soft linen dress with blue flowers on it. Her little fingers were still curled from when she had been holding the basket moments before her death.

I didn't need to read an article online about who she was to know that she had been the flower girl at the wedding they were going home from.

The blood splattered on her body did nothing to take away from her beauty, and in that corpse lying on the side of the road I could see that she had never been more beautiful than in the hours before I took her life.

I could see her walking down the aisle, smiling. Carefree, excited to be a part of something much bigger than she could understand. I could see—no, I could feel the people in the pews in awe of how beautiful she looked, the mothers hoping one day their children could look as beautiful.

I could see her dark hair bouncing up and down and see her dress sway with each step, with each time she reached into the basket to throw petals. I could see her chubby cheeks, full of life and energy and possibility.

I could see her finding her mother somewhere in the crowd, and smiling at her. Her mother smiling back, full of pride at how adorable her daughter was, imagining how she would look at her own wedding, and thinking how lucky and special the man who captured her perfect angel's heart would have to be.

And she *would have* been beautiful at her own wedding. And he *would have* been special and lucky, if not for me.

But they had no idea in that moment of elation, a moment that would never end in their hearts, that there was a monster somewhere out there drinking up and arguing stupid bullshit at a crappy house party, getting ready to slay her.

They didn't know I existed, but in the coming hours, I would haunt the mother's mind for the rest of her life.

I never wanted to wink out of existence more than in that moment when I saw her lying on the side of the road. I didn't exactly want to die; I don't think I was even cognizant enough to think in those terms. I more wanted to just cease to be.

My eyes moved from her lifeless corpse and traced the trail of blood to where her head lay. It was face up, and rested on a nest of curly brown hair. It seemed to be made of wax, wax from heaven, because even in the crooked stillness of death it was the face of an angel.

My mind wanted to trick me into thinking this was all one big hoax, that the accident hadn't actually been that bad. That this body lying before my eyes wasn't real, that it was someone's idea of a sick joke.

But deep down in my heart, I knew the truth. Deep down in my heart, I knew the monster I was.

I didn't break out of my trance until I felt cold steel being wrapped around my wrists. I heard the officer read me my rights, and wondered why he couldn't just gun me down right then and there in front of all of these people.

*

The person that came up with the old adage of "sticks and stones may break my bones, but words will never hurt me" obviously never faced an entire courthouse that hated them.

From the judge, to the jury, to even my own damn lawyer, they all hated me.

I almost saw the jury wanting to wince with every word my lawyer spouted out as my defense.

But worst of all was facing the family.

Even the driver was there, and had his arm in a cast. He said the doctor told him his arm would probably never be the same, but that that was nothing compared to what I did to the sweet little girl that everyone who met fell in love with.

That includes me, by the way.

I'm her killer, though, so I guess that doesn't mean jackshit, does it?

*

Today is my birthday, and next week I have my last court appearance. I won't be there because I had Glenda bring me a cake. It's chocolate with vanilla frosting.

I asked her to bake a shoelace into it.

I've written this note as a confession, to make amends with myself, and with Him. I hope whoever finds it publicizes it somehow, but I don't expect anyone to find it in their heart to forgive me. If they did, they'd be fresh out of forgiveness. Better to save it for someone who deserves it.

I'm going to go now and celebrate my birthday. It's my last one, after all.

I'm sorry. Goodbye.

BOARD OF DOOM

Part I: Setup & Instructions

"Board of Doom," Cory said, reading the title of the game.

Stanley found it in his grandmother's attic last week. After she passed away the family had rummaged through her house and he had been allowed to keep this old game.

Cory threw the lid onto the table and scoffed. "Stupid name, not even scary."

Larry snatched up the lid to take a look at it. "No one is scared of it, you dipshit."

"They're clearly trying to make it look scary, and it's not, whiz kid." Cory fired back.

BOARD of DOOM was written in red letters that oozed down the cover of the game like blood, so Cory was on the right track. There was also a woman, drawn in the old-timey style that Larry had seen before in his father's old Western comic book collection, with her mouth slightly agape in the middle of a gasp. Her left hand was coming up to her mouth, and her green eyes swam with worry. She was in the dungeon of a castle, and behind her was a doorway decorated with spikes leading to a flight of stairs. At the top, two ominous red eyes glared out from the darkness.

"Spooky," Larry said, grinning. He flipped the lid over to where the instructions were written.

Larry was in the gifted classes a year ahead of his grade, had built his own computer last summer, and looked every bit the part of a whiz kid. He even wore thick-rimmed glasses, and as such, the group always expected him to do the brainy stuff, including anything that had to do with reading.

"How many people can play?" Sheila asked, cracking open a can of orange soda.

"Board of Doom is a game for 2-4 people," Larry announced.

"Awesome," Stanley said.

This was what the four kids who lived between Florence Ave and Oakhill Lane did on summer days. They gathered in the basement of old man Gunther's house—which had been left abandoned since he died, but everyone in the neighborhood still referred to it as his house—and played board games and card games. Usually it was Monopoly or Go Fish, but occasionally they liked to switch it up.

Summer was winding down and they'd all be in the 7th grade (except for Larry, who would be in 8th grade) in two weeks and bogged down with homework, so they figured they'd test the game out to see if it'd make the cut to be a regular addition next summer break.

From what they could tell, it looked promising. The board had an intricate design, colorful but not quite cheerful so that it still kept up with its name. There was a basic squared path, made up of 26 spaces. Each space was white, red, blue, or yellow. Designed around the spaces, and drawn in the same fashion as the front cover of the game, were weapons like swords and axes, goblin creatures, and strange symbols that were vaguely satanic without being satanic.

"Alright," Larry said, "Rule #1. Each player selects a game piece and puts it in the START space."

Stanley had taken the brass figures out of their pouch and strewn them on the coffee table, around the game board, so they could all see them.

There was a cowboy wielding two pistols, a wizard with a beard that reached down to his waist, an imp holding a bag over its shoulder, a witch riding a broom while cackling, and a knight with a heavy sword and shield.

There were six of them, but Cory's and Stanley's fingers clashed above the cowboy as they both reached for it. Their eyes locked.

"My arm moved first," Cory said.

"It's my game, stupid ass, which means I *saw* it first," Stanley fired back.

"You're too much of a chicken to be the cowboy," Cory returned, scowling.

Stan's brows furrowed. "I'm the cowboy——"

"No, I *am*——"

"Guys, guys! Settle down," Larry said.

They both stopped shouting, but kept their eyes locked on one another.

Larry looked over at Sheila, and she rolled her eyes. Turning back to the boys, Larry said, "Core, just let him be the cowboy. It's his game, pick a different figure."

"No, I want to be the cowboy. I don't care if it's his game."

"Then you're not playing, jerkoff!" Stan said, getting out of his chair and his face turning red.

"Stan, chill out!" Larry said, waving his hand at him.

He reached into the box and pulled out the die. "Fine, since you're both being babies about it, why don't you guys roll to see who gets to play the cowboy."

Cory crossed his arms in front of his chest, which pushed his fatboy boobs up, and let out a puff of air through his nostrils.

"Come on, Cory, stop being an ass-munch," Larry said.

The way Larry said *ass-munch* always got him, and Cory couldn't help but chuckle. He held his hand out for Larry to give him the die.

Larry turned to Stanley, "You cool with this, Stan?"

Stanley nodded and said, "Yeah, yeah."

Larry handed Cory the die.

"Freakin' baby," Sheila whispered, intentionally loud enough for Cory to hear.

He shot her a dirty glare, and she responded by sticking her tongue out at him.

Cory rolled a 2, and let out a puff of air.

Laughing, Stan picked the die up and rolled. 6.

The group laughed, except for Cory.

"Looks like I'm the cowboy," Stanley said, placing the figure into the purple space labeled START.

"Whatever, cowboys are stupid and lame, anyway."

Cory scanned the figures remaining on the table and settled on the knight. He placed it next to Stanley's cowboy, and then tried smacking the figure away with the back of his hand. The figure didn't go flying the way he expected it to, instead it remained where it was, as if glued to the board, and the metal slamming against his knuckles made him yelp out in pain.

They all laughed at him again.

"What the hell," he said, turning away from the group and licking his reddening knuckles.

"I guess metal beats fat," Stanley said.

Sheila laughed harder and reached over the table with her fist clenched, and they fist-bumped.

Trying not to laugh any harder himself, Larry said, "Come on guys, lay off him already."

Sheila and Stan shared one last giggle, then settled down as per his order.

Cory turned back to the group and looked at the brass figure with a reproachful eye as if it were a kid on the playground that had sucker-punched him. He was ready to flip the damn table over and storm out of the house.

Screw this game. He thought, but the part of his mind that still thought the game might be fun made him stay put.

"Alright, alright, Sheila, pick your piece," Larry said, turning the group's attention back to the game. "I'll pick last."

Sheila's hand hovered over the four remaining pieces, and settled on the imp. She picked it up and looked at it closely. It had little fangs sticking out from the top lip and tiny boots on its feet. It was supposed to look devilish, but it was kind of cute in design.

"I'll take the little guy," she said, dropping it into the starting zone next to Cory and Stanley's pieces.

"Alright, then I'll take him," Larry said, placing the wizard in front of the other game pieces.

The leader in real life and the leader in games, too. Nothing changed.

"Okay, now what?" Cory asked.

Larry read the next step. "Next, we pick the appropriate character card from the character deck."

He put the lid to the side and then took out the character deck from the box. He shuffled through it until he found the right cards. The cards were done in trading card style; they had a drawing of the character and then a small paragraph at the bottom about their ability.

Larry handed the cards out, and then picked the lid back up and continued reading the instructions. "If there are any first time players—so all of us—each player reads their character card out loud to the rest of the group."

He put the lid to the side. "Mine says: The wizard has the ability to reroll any die roll, once per game. This can even be used to force other players to reroll."

"Oh my God, of course whiz kid gets the total bullshit one," Cory said in frustration.

Larry's eyebrows knitted together. "Quit complainin' and read yours."

Cory read his card to himself first. His face turned red with anger. "Fuck this game."

Stanley tilted his head back and let out a shriek of laughter. "What is it? What does it say? You have to tell us."

"The knight's movements are all reduced by 1," Cory said, and bent the card down the middle.

Sheila and Stanley began to laugh, and as much as Larry tried to fight it, he couldn't hold it in and started laughing too.

Cory slammed the card on the table and crossed his arms. "I'm not playing."

"Fine, then don't, crybaby," Larry said, and then to Stanley said, "you go next."

Stanley let out one final fit of laughter and then cleared his throat. He held the card close to his eyes to read it. He needed glasses, but he refused to wear the ones hanging from the collar of his shirt because he would rather deal with the strain on his eyeballs than be a four-eyes dweeb. "The cowboy gets extra damage added to all of his weapons."

He looked around the group and shrugged.

"Sheila," Larry said to her.

Sheila read hers. "Once per game, the imp can steal another player's turn."

"Alright, we all read our powers," Larry said. He turned to Cory. "You're still not playing?"

"No, this game is stupid," Cory spat.

"There's more to your card than what you read," Larry said. "It's not all bad."

Cory grabbed the card from Larry and finished reading the knight's description. He grinned when he read the second part of his character's ability. "Oh, you're right."

"Read it out loud, dummy," Sheila said.

Cory shot her a dirty look and then read it aloud. "The knight can roll 3 times on the same turn, once per game. The knight also gets the first turn at the beginning of every game."

"So are you playing now?" Stanley asked.

"No, I don't want to play with you guys." Cory threw the card back in the box.

"Fine, then just watch us have fun while you have your thumb up your ass," Larry scolded.

Cory turned away from them, but kept his focus out the corner of his eye. He really did want to play; he just didn't want to admit it. The game had an aura to it the moment they opened the box. A pull almost, a pull of mystery and danger.

The danger part, they'd come to find out was real. All too real.

*

Old Man Gunther's house sat in a lonely corner of town, on a hilltop surrounded by shrubs and tall oak trees, just the way the old man had liked it when he was still alive. It kept the nosy neighbors from out of sight since the house could hardly be seen from the quiet town below, and this was also what made it an ideal hangout.

It wasn't spooky, despite being old and abandoned, because Gunther and his wife had kept it spick-and-span throughout their lifetime. Even after his wife died, he had kept up with the maintenance. Painting it every end of summer, fixing up the deck, and showing the house general tender love and care.

But as the children read their cards to one another in the basement, a fog began to surround it. It was thick and almost black, and looked more like clouds filled with rain, but moved in a haze the way fog did in old horror movies.

No one from town could see it over the hill, but it had formed the moment the game pieces were put on the board because the rules of the game stated that—

*

"—the game cannot stop being played until someone wins." Larry read the next part of the instructions. "The player who reaches the top of Castle Light is declared the winner."

Their eyes all hovered over the end of the board, where there was a ray of sunshine beaming down on a castle surrounded by a field of purple flowers. Drawn into the image of the layers of the castle were three spaces, which presumably meant a player who landed on the bottom level of the castle would have to roll a 2 or higher to win the game. Simple enough.

"Okay, it says to decide who goes first, we roll. Highest number wins, unless the knight is in play, in which case the knight goes first and the person to his or her left goes next, and so on." Larry said.

"But I'm not playing," Cory said, and got out of his chair. "Actually, I'm going home."

He grabbed a bag of pretzels—family size— and headed up the stairs, marching up in dramatic fashion, hoping and waiting they'd all shout for him to come back and play. He felt a wave of disappointment when he reached the last step and no one had made a peep.

Stanley and Larry looked at one another, and both rolled their eyes.

"Alright, well, since there's only three of us, let's roll to see who goes first." Larry said.

He picked up the die and threw it on the board. 4.

Sheila rolled next. 6.

"Yeah! Looks like I'm first unless you roll a 6, too, Stan."

Stan grabbed the die and rolled a 5.

"So I'm first, and then Larry since he's to my left," Sheila said, picking up the die from the board.

Each turn the player rolled one die for movement, and there were 26 spaces in total on the board, which meant that a player who rolled five 6's in a row would win the game.

Sheila rolled the die, and it came up a 5. Grinning with delight, she wrapped two fingers around the little imp's head. She tried picking it up, but it wouldn't budge.

"Hm," she said.

"What?" Stanley asked.

"It's stuck, it won't move." She tried again, with some more muscle this time, but it remained in place. Something was keeping it from moving.

"Must be magnets," Larry said.

Although, the box said nothing about the game being magnetized. Also, that wouldn't explain why hers specifically wouldn't move. The rules of the game were that if the knight were in play that player would be the first to go, but how would the board know which pieces to magnetize and which not to?

A chip, perhaps?

Larry looked at the cover, which was between his and Sheila's chair, at the woman that was perpetually gasping in horror in old 1940s movie poster style. That technology didn't exist back then. He didn't think so, at least.

"I guess the game knows who we picked," Stanley said, vocalizing what Larry had been thinking. "So Cory has to play."

The answer didn't suffice Larry, but he nodded. "Yeah, I'll go get him. He just left, he couldn't have gotten too far."

Sheila picked up her soda and looked out the window. "Was it supposed to be foggy today?"

Larry shrugged, so did Stanley.

"I'll be back," Larry said, and headed up the stairs after Cory.

*

This isn't fog was the first thing that sprung to his mind when he stepped into the thick, gray clouds. For one thing, it didn't spread out in wisps the way even the heaviest of fog did. No, whatever this was continued surrounding him with no giving way where he stood, so that he was surrounded by the fluff. Not exactly constricted by it, but it wrapped around him tight enough to give off the illusion of being held in place.

What kind of prank are those jerks playing on me? was his second thought.

He had only stepped a couple of paces into the fog, maybe ten or fifteen, so he could turn back, but there was something in this haze that made him stay. A mental block of sorts.

The clouds in front of him began to swirl like they were being spun into a tornado by an unseen force—there wasn't even any wind or momentum to it, it was just happening. The swirl took the shape of a skull, and out from between the clouds two red eyes glared at him.

The Keeper of the Board.

Cory didn't know why that name came to him, but it did, and he knew that was the name of the entity he was face-to-face with.

"No one leaves the game until there is a victor," the voice boomed out from every direction, "Turn back and play."

Cory wanted to make a snarky remark, insult this thing's mother or something along those lines, but he was too tantalized. The moment was surreal, and bigger than his mouth, he found.

So instead, in a voice as low as a mouse's squeak, he said, "Wha-what if I don't?"

The Keeper's jaw moved in a way that twisted its features into a grin, and then it said, "All who have joined the game will be smitten."

"What do you-you mean?" Cory asked, and took two steps backward—back toward Old Man Gunther's house. Suddenly he was ready to roll dice.

"Exactly what I've said, child. If you don't turn back to finish the game you and your friends started, all four of you will pay with your lives."

As if to show him he could do it, as if to put an exclamation point on the statement, a bolt of lightning came down from the sky. Cory jumped as the blue light struck the grass between him and the Keeper, burning and frizzling it.

There was no fight in him after this. He screamed, and ran through the clouds, heading back to his friends.

*

Larry saw him dashing out of the dark clouds and across the lawn straight at him with no signs of slowing down. He wasn't quick enough to get out of the way, and Cory crashed into him. His jiggly body against his felt like a water mattress, and then a shock of pain shot up his ass as he slammed against the ground.

Even though Cory outweighed him by at least thirty pounds, he had lost balance and fallen too. Out of breath and on all fours on the grass he said to Larry, "Don't go in there, man."

Larry sat up and straightened his glasses on his face. "Slow down, slow down. What the hell are you talking about?"

Cory's face scrunched up in frustration, and he threw an arm into the air like a whip. "You don't see that crap surrounding Old Man Gunther's house?"

He looked around, and now that Cory had drawn attention to it, he noticed that it wasn't anything like regular fog. No, this was more of a ring of dark clouds surrounding the house, leaving only a few feet of the yard cleared of it.

Something told him that the clouds didn't extend very far from the house, and the rest of town wasn't experiencing this phenomenon.

Cory got up and wiped dirt and grass off of his hands and pants. "I saw something in there."

Larry got up, too. "What?"

"I went into the clouds, and I met the Keeper."

"Keeper?" Larry shook his head. "Jesus man, did you bump your head or something?"

"Don't play stupid, whiz kid," Cory said, and stamped closer to him, so close their noses were only inches apart from each other, "You know what's happening—that fucking stupid game Stanley brought is doing this."

Larry took in a deep breath. He was right; for once Cory was right. He was trying to convince himself that nothing weird was going on, as if that somehow would make this all go away. Larry read a lot of science fiction comic books, enough to know that the clouds and the game board were connected. It was too coincidental to be coincidental, as Yogi Berra had said.

"The Keeper of the Board said we can't leave until the game ends," Cory looked down at the plastic watch on his wrist, "and I have to be home for dinner in half an hour. So let's turn back and go play."

Larry nodded, and they both headed back into the house.

*

127

At the top of the steps leading into the basement, Cory put a hand on Larry's shoulder. He had calmed down. The nerves from meeting the Keeper had died off, and he was able to speak without yelling. In a hushed voice, he said, "Larry, are we going to tell them?"

"Tell them what? That the game is haunted and we can't leave until we finish the game?" Larry whispered back.

Cory thought of the blue lightning bolt and the Keeper's threat to smite them all. He hadn't told Larry about that yet, but he had seen enough to know that the game might kill them. That the "Doom" in "Board of Doom" was more than just a word.

"Yeah," Cory said. "I don't want to scare Stanley, you know how much of a wimp he is. He might not want to play."

Larry didn't bother pointing out that he had been the one to quit the game before it started. There were more important things to discuss. Brushing Cory's hand off his shoulder and turning back toward the stairs, he said, "I don't know."

Before he could move again, Cory grabbed his shoulder.

"What, man?"

"I got one more thing to tell you." Cory's face went pale.

"Go ahead."

"We might be playing for our lives," Cory said, and coughed to clear his throat.

"What the hell makes you say that?" Larry said it louder than he intended.

Cory saw the fear in his eyes. The big stupid glasses magnifying them on his face didn't help the situation. If Larry, their unofficial leader, was shaken up, then it was with good reason. That was what these geeks operated on, after all, reason and logic.

"The Keeper said we have to finish the game, or else we'll all get smitten. He shot down a bolt of lightning near my feet to show he wasn't kidding around."

"Are you yanking my chain, Core?"

Cory shook his head. "No way man. Why do you think I was running out of the clouds? I was freaked out."

Larry sighed. "I'll tell them, then."

"Why you? I can tell them."

"They won't believe you."

"What the hell? Why not?" Now Cory was raising his voice.

"Because you're constantly spinning tales to us, that's why. I'll tell them everything, I'll tell them I saw the Keeper." Larry turned back and went down the stairs.

"Hold on! What lies have I told?"

Larry rolled his eyes and half-turned to face him. "Like when you told us you kissed Melissa Sanderson under the mistletoe last Christmas."

"What! I did," he was yelling now, but Larry ignored him and descended the stairs.

Following behind him, he said, "Dude! I did!"

*

When they came down the stairs, the first thing Stanley noticed was that Larry's face was long and drained of color. Sheila had noticed it too, because when he glanced over at her, he saw her fidgeting in her chair. If Larry was worried about something, then there was a reason they all should be worried. Stan's mouth felt dry suddenly.

Larry stopped over the table, and Cory plopped down into the lawn chair. The plastic frame creaked underneath the weight.

Larry ran his hands through his hair, and then exhaled before saying: "Okay, guys… hear me out."

"Did Cory call his mom? He did, didn't he?" Stanley stood up, kicking the chair out behind him and clenching his fists.

"What?" Cory fired back, and also got up with his fists clenched.

Stanley was the runt of the group, but he was also like a shaken can of soda when it came to Cory's shenanigans and he could only contain the pressure for so long.

"Guys, guys, settle down!" Larry put his hand on Cory's chest and pushed him back into the chair. To Stan, he said, "It has nothing to do with that. Sit down."

Stan did as he was told.

"What is it then? Cops?" Sheila asked, ready to grab her schoolbag and head up the stairs if the answer was yes.

"No, it's not that. We're not in trouble—"

"Yet," Cory interjected.

Larry shot him a glare that made him drop his eyes to the ground and shrink back in his chair. He grumbled something under his breath, either an apology or an insult, Larry wasn't sure, but it didn't matter.

"The game." He jutted his chin toward the board where the brass pieces patiently waited for their moves. "It's haunted, or something."

"Oh God," Sheila groaned and her body relaxed, "so Cory is dragging you into his stupid jokes now?"

"We're not joking, dumbo," Cory blurted out.

"Cory, shut *up*." He waved his hand at him. "It's not a joke guys. That's why Sheila's piece can't be moved from where it is. That's why there's suddenly fog out there when we've never gotten that weather in town before."

He shook his head and said to Cory, "Maybe you should tell them what happened."

"I went into the fog and met the Keeper of the Board. He was this giant skull made of fog with glowing red eyes. He can shoot lightning."

Stanley wanted so badly to laugh, but the look on Larry's face suggested he believed every word. If Larry believed it, then that meant Larry had seen something out there that made it possible Cory wasn't just making things up as usual.

"We have to play the game or we'll all be struck by lightning," Cory saw the look in their eyes, and they finally all believed him.

Of the most unbelievable events he ever told, this one was the most farfetched, but it was the one that had them hanging on his every word. He couldn't help but feel the smallest inkling of triumph swim through him.

"Larry...?" Sheila muttered. Her voice was small and girlish. She was curled into a ball on her chair with her knees pressed up against her chest. A far cry from her usual Tomboyish demeanor.

Larry sat down in his chair next to her and picked up the die. "We're not messing around. I saw the fog out there, it's not really fog."

"Then what is it?" Stanley asked.

"It's like," Larry paused to try to find the words, "it's like a barrier to keep us locked in with the game."

Cory stuck his hand out, palm open. "Give me the die. Let's play this stupid game and get it over with."

Larry nodded and dropped the die into his hand. He shook the die in his closed fist and then let it roll across the table. 4.

Before he could even move his hand to grab the brass figure, it slid on its own. It slid from behind the other three figures and then went across the board and landed on the appropriate space—space 3, which was blank.

"The knight loses one from its movement rolls." Cory reminded them.

This time, it wasn't funny though.

All four of the kids looked at one another, and they all silently agreed at the oddity and spookiness of it all.

Stanley was next. He picked up the die and rolled it. The cowboy moved on his own as well, his two trusty pistols pointed in front of him as he slid past the knight figure.

Unlike the space where Cory's figure had stopped, this spot was red and had the command: "Pick Up a Red Card" on it.

In the middle of the board were three decks of cards. Each was a different color: red, blue, and yellow.

"Did you guys set these up while we were out there?" Larry asked, hoping the answer was yes.

Sheila and Stanley looked at one another and shook their heads.

"Fucking ghosts," Cory said, "are you guys happy? We could be playing Monopoly instead."

Larry shot him a dirty glance, but it didn't work anymore because Cory could see the fear behind it. He was forcing it, trying to keep himself cool for the group, instead of just being cool as he usually was.

"Alright," Larry said, "pick up a card and read it to us."

Stanley grabbed the top card on the deck and read what was written: "Quicksand: The player cannot move unless he or she rolls a 1, 3, or 6 on their next turn. If the player is stuck for more than 3 turns, the Death Worm will devour him/her."

He put the card down in front of him with a deep inhalation of air. "Guys, I don't think I want to play."

"None of us do, bonehead, but we don't have a choice," Cory said. "Come on, Sheila, go."

"Look, there are 26 spots, which means the game can end in less than 5 turns if someone gets lucky. You guys are making this seem more difficult than it actually is." Larry said.

"Yeah, well, you didn't see the Keeper of the Board, Larry. You didn't almost get fried by his lightning bolt. You're not the one stuck in quicksand, are you?" Cory said, getting out of his chair.

"I haven't taken a turn yet, you moron," Larry said, also standing up.

"I'm taking my turn." Sheila tugged Larry by the forearm, and he sat back down.

Cory did too, but neither one wanted to break eye contact first. They had only gotten into one fistfight since they had been friends, and it had been two summers ago before Cory hit his growth spurt and had been three inches shorter than Larry at the time. Now they were closer in height, but Cory had gained about fifteen pounds since then.

Neither one of them knew who would come out victorious if they had to duke it out again.

Sheila grabbed the die and rolled before anything else could happen between them.

The die tumbled across the board and came up a five. The imp moved along the board and stopped at a blank space. Collectively the group breathed a sigh of relief.

"Your turn, fearless leader," Cory taunted.

Larry ignored him and rolled the die.

2.

"Shit," he said, and thought about his character ability. He could reroll, but it was too soon; the game had just started.

The wizard moved two spaces, to a blue space with the same command to pick up a card, only from the blue deck.

"Good job," Cory said.

Larry hovered his hand over the cards, and for a second wondered what would happen if he didn't pick one up. Probably the same thing that happened when Sheila tried rolling when Cory wasn't going to play. The board had somehow tied their souls into the game. As stupid as that sounded to him, that was likely what was going on.

And if he tried picking up a different colored card than the one the space commanded him to?

You didn't almost get fried by his lightning bolt... He heard Cory say in his mind.

Larry had a hunch that if he tried outsmarting the game, the Keeper wouldn't almost fry him, he'd actually hit his mark.

He picked up the blue card and read it to the group. "*Light Shield: If you land on a red spot, you can use this card to get out of it and move ahead 2 spaces.*"

Back to Cory, back to the knight in shining armor. He rolled.

6.

Which meant the knight moved 5 spaces across the board when the knight's handicap was taken into account. Another blank space. "If I can get through this stupid game hitting all blank spaces I'll be happy about that."

"Yeah," Larry said, nodding. "Come on, Stan, roll a 1, 3, or 6 to get out of the quicksand."

Stanley's face was paper white and his fingers shook as he curled his hand around the die. Holding his breath, he let the die roll across the board.

2.

Drats. The color in his face further drained.

"Don't worry, next turn," Sheila said, and patted him on the shoulder.

He didn't respond, though, just nodded and then looked down at the board with wide eyes. Something wasn't right. Something in the air around him had changed since he drew the quicksand card.

Sheila took her turn and rolled a six. The imp moved and landed on a blue spot. She read the card: "Horn of the Unicorn: Add 3 to your next roll."

They all celebrated in silence. Sheila's last two rolls had been great, and if her next one kept up with the pattern she'd be past the halfway mark, on only turn 2.

"Don't roll another two, ding-a-ling," Cory said before Larry took his turn.

"Shut up," Larry said, and let the die fly out of his hand.

4.

The wizard moved to the red spot where Stanley's cowboy was stuck.

"Tough luck, leader," Cory said.

"I don't know why you're turning this into a joke, Cory."

Before picking up the red card, he looked over at Stanley in an effort to console him. To tell him, *don't worry bud, we're both in the same jam now.* But something was off.

Not just that his best friend looked the color of uncooked rice, but he appeared smaller. The top of the coffee table they were playing on was covering the top part of his *Duck Tales* t-shirt, where normally it'd be a little above his waist. It was as if he was shrinking.

No, not shrinking. *Sinking.*

"Stan?" He didn't mean to vocalize it, but the shock sent it sputtering out from between his lips.

This drew the attention of Sheila and Cory, and Stan winced backward at their gazes. It only took a second for the other two to notice that he was lower than usual.

"What?" Stanley asked.

"Quicksand," Cory said it under his breath, but the others heard it.

Stanley looked down at his chair, and half of all four of the chair's legs were buried underneath sand. The sand extended beyond the chair a couple of feet, as if a small sandbank had formed when they hadn't been looking.

Stan watched it move, sifting downward as if alive, waiting to consume him. Underneath the seat of his chair, in the middle of this patch of quicksand, was an impossible sinkhole. The floorboards of the basement had been replaced somehow, magic perhaps, and now he was on top of a death trap.

As that thought passed through his mind, he could suddenly hear the heartbeat of something underneath his feet. Something big, something scary. Something hungry.

The Death Worm.

He was in the clutches of the Board of Doom. They all were.

Part II: Playtime

They had all seen the sand surrounding Stanley's chair, and they all knew what they were in for. The game wasn't just a haunted game; it was a part of their reality now.

Larry gulped, and looked at the red card in his hand. "*The Mask of the Dead has attached itself to you. Skip your next turn.*"

He felt both a gush of relief and guilt at his draw. It was going to suck to lose a turn, but he wasn't in any danger the way Stanley was, so he wasn't going to use the Light Shield. Not yet, not until the game threatened to do something like *devour* him.

That was the conclusion of turn 2, and now the rotation was back to Cory. He took in a deep breath, grabbed the die and threw it across the board. 5.

The knight moved the 4 spaces, taking into account the character's movement deficit, and landed on a corner spot on the board. Cory picked up from the blue deck and read his card. "*Magic Blast: this card can be used to rid any red card effect out of the game.*"

"Use it on Stan's quicksand card," Larry commanded.

"No," Cory fired. "It's my card, I'll use it when I want to."

"You're just going to let Stanley sit in the quicksand another turn?" Larry was ready to get up and go to blows with him. He was at his nerve's end now.

"Yeah, you stupid ass. He has two more turns before he gets devoured, I'll play it if he doesn't get out of the sand this turn."

Larry sat back in his chair, even though he was angrier now. Cory was awful at every game they played—whether it was wallball or Mario Kart—but right now he was keeping a cooler head than him, and it was making this all a worse experience.

"Fine," Larry muttered. "Stan, you cool with that?"

Stan nodded. His movement was so stiff they all expected his neck to creak.

"Okay, then," Larry said, and pushed the die across the table, closer to Stan. "Go ahead and roll."

Stan picked up the die and rolled. 5.

"Dammit," Cory said, and held up his blue card. "How do I use this thing?"

He turned to Larry, who shrugged and said, "I don't know... just think it. Or read the card and say you're going to use it or something."

"Fine. I'm going to use my blue card. You hear that game? You hear that, Keeper? You hear that, stupid worm monster?"

They sat there for a few moments. Nothing happened.

Cory twiddled his thumbs while Stan's color further drained out of his face.

Maybe we can't use this card like this. Larry thought.

Then he looked underneath the table, where Stan's chair was to see if the quicksand was still there. It was, nothing had changed on that side of the table, where Cory was, something did.

"Core," he said. As much as he enjoyed giving Cory a hard time, this wasn't the same. This wasn't like the time at summer camp when Larry stuck a garter snake inside of Cory's sleeping bag and he ran out of the cabin screaming the top of his head off, no, the danger here was real.

"What?" Cory said, his eyes bugged out.

"Look at your feet." Larry said.

Cory looked down, and in the moment it took him to realize that there was sand under *his* feet now, something grabbed him by the ankles —*the Board of Doom*, the thought quickly flashed in his head—and pulled him into the sand.

He screamed. Larry jumped out of his seat and tried to grab him, but he was too slow. Instead, he smacked against the empty chair and sent it flying as his arms wrapped around nothing but air.

Larry stood over the sandbank. The hole was pulling in sand from the outer edges and filling itself up. He watched as the opening between this world and whatever world Cory had been sucked into closed.

"Core! Cory! Cory!"

Sheila ran around the table and wrapped her arms around his waist, and pulled him back, away from the quicksand. "Larry, get a hold of yourself."

Larry's knees went weak, and he sat down on the floor. Sheila followed him and kneeled down beside him, patting his back.

He finally took his eyes away from the sand once the hole was completely sealed and the sand stopped moving, and they met Sheila's eyes.

"What if he's dead?"

She had never seen Larry even come close to crying. Well, only when he had fallen out of the tree two summers ago, but that was understandable, and now he was on the verge of tears because their friend might be dead.

"He's not, Larry," she said, and hugged him. She didn't know for sure, but she would have said anything at that moment to keep him from crying. "Cory's not dead, okay?"

"Guys," Stan said. He was still in his chair, held in place by the force of the game and still sitting in the quicksand, but some of the color was returning to his face. "Guys, look."

Both Larry and Sheila looked to where he pointed. There was a luminescent aura surrounding the brass knight figure, making the shiny piece even shinier.

"I don't think he's dead," Stan said. "I think... I think he got sent to fight the Death Worm for me."

Larry sat up, and Sheila let go of him. He fixed his glasses on his face, which had gone crooked when he jumped for Cory. "Holy crap, Stan, you might be right."

He crawled over to the patch of sand and yelled down into it. "Cory! Can you hear me?"

*

Cory could hear him, loud and clear, as if he were everywhere all at once. It was similar to the voice of the Keeper, only it was Larry's coming through.

He didn't know where the hell he was, but he knew he got here by the force that dragged him through the sandbank.

All around him was sand, but it wasn't like the slideshow of Mr. Huxley's Spring Break trip to Utah he had bored the entire 4th-period class with. No, this was a room made entirely of sand, the walls, the floor, the ceiling, everything.

In the distance, maybe a half mile away, there was sand pouring down into the room like a waterfall.

A sandfall, he thought, and chuckled at the cleverness.

Besides the sandfall, there were tiny sand geysers in every direction he looked.

Larry was still yelling at him from the world above, and Cory couldn't decide if the constant hissing the sand geysers made or his yelling was more annoying. He cupped his hands around his mouth and yelled up into the room, "Shut up, Larry! Your voice is shaking the damn walls."

It was. With each word Larry had been saying, the walls surrounding him had spilled some of their grains down to the ground, adding to the mounds of sand already formed at their bases.

Larry's voice stopped for a second, and then it came back, softer this time. "Cory, where are you?"

"In some sandy room," he said back.

This way of communicating made Cory feel strange, like talking to someone on the phone that's in the room right next door.

"Is there an exit?"

Cory scanned the room left and right, and then spun in a circle. Nothing but sand, sand, and more sand.

"No, man, no exit. I'm going to go look for one," he said, and started walking.

He was happy to find that the sand wasn't any different than the sand at the beach (which he hated going to because he didn't like taking his shirt off) and not quicksand. He took a couple of steps, then felt a small rumble.

"Uh-oh," he said, and took another step.

The rumbling got bigger. The happiness was quickly replaced by worry.

Another step.

A bigger rumble.

He wanted to run, but then thought better of it because maybe it was his steps that were causing it. He stopped, and looked around for any signs of anything else that might be doing it.

The rumbling turned into shaking, first the floor shook, and then the entire room.

Sand began to blast all over the place as if he were caught in a giant salt shaker. It shot up from the ground, blasted out of the walls, and came down from the unseen ceiling.

Oh crap, oh crap.

The entire room was about to fall in on him; he had fucked with the Death Worm and was about to become its lunch.

I knew I shouldn't have listened to that friggin' four-eyes was his last thought before the sand in front of him exploded into the air and a giant hole opened.

*

Larry watched the sand begin to move again, and bad thoughts raced through his mind. His heart felt like it was going to leap out of his chest. When they heard the sound of a small bang, he and Sheila had stepped back from the sand, but they were still watching intently.

Sheila gripped his shoulder, digging her short nails into his skin. He could hear her chewing on the nails of her other hand.

"What's going on?" she asked him, as if he'd know.

He glanced over at the knight on the board, and it was still glowing. That was good. He assumed that as long as the game piece was glowing, that meant Cory was still alive.

"I don't know," he whispered to her. Then toward the quicksand, toward Cory, he shouted, "Cory, you alright?"

No response.

Sheila dug her nails deeper into his shoulder. Now it was uncomfortable, and Larry reached up and pulled her cold hand off of his shoulder and held it.

*

Cory closed his eyes and held his arms in front of his face to shield himself from getting sand into them. When he felt the pelting of the grains slow, he put his arms down and saw the monstrosity that stared back at him.

Well... he wasn't sure if it stared back at him necessarily, because the giant worm had no eyes, but its mouth was pointed at him. It had the body of and wiggled like an earthworm, but somewhere at the top of what would be considered the monster's head was a mouth large enough to eat a van in one swallow.

It was open, exposing teeth that went around the entirety of the mouth in a circle, like an inverted buzzsaw.

Despite the hideous sight, Cory felt unmoved. He wasn't sure why he felt so calm and collected, but he was glad he did, because there was no way he was returning to the others with his pants full of crap. They'd never let him live that down.

Besides the worm, Cory could feel a familiar presence somewhere in the room. It wasn't Larry's; this was an ominous presence that seemed to be daring him somehow.

"So you're the thing that wants to eat Stanley, huh?" Cory said, and balled his fists.

The Death Worm's mouth stretched wider, exposing more of the sharp teeth, but Cory's newfound bravado remained.

This isn't me. I'm not actually here, I'm not this brave.

It felt strange to be brave considering he lived most of his life *pretending* to be brave, and now here he was faced with an actual monster, and was unmoved. He was ready to... ready to what?

I'm ready to blast you into smithereens, you ugly shit.

The worm wiggled up, revealing more of its smooth, pink body, and then curled so its head and mouth was pointed straight at the 12-year-old chubby kid.

"Come on, come get me, ugly!" Cory taunted it.

The ominous presence grew stronger, and he knew what it was. In the seconds before the worm lunged out at him, he knew the presence was the Keeper.

Of course, the Keeper controlled everything within the purple fog.

The worm lunged at him, mouth stretching wider and wider the closer it zoomed toward him.

The bravado escaped out of Cory, and the reality of the situation hit him. He felt his legs turn to cooked spaghetti, then he was yelling at the top of his lungs.

The mouth drew in closer, closer, so close he could smell the worm's breath.

His yelling grew louder the less distance there was between them.

He yelled so loud that his ears began to ring and his vision went away, and he saw nothing but whiteness.

This must be death, he thought.

Then he felt something reach inside of him, something like a hand, and pull out an essence, something like power.

The whiteness went away, and he saw a ray of light shoot out from his chest and hit the Death Worm right in the mouth.

Cory had been screaming so loud and so long that his lungs hurt, but now that he saw the worm recoil in pain from the blast, he screamed louder. His lungs felt like they were being punctured by a harpoon, but it didn't matter, because the louder he screamed, the bigger the light got.

The light shot through the Death Worm, piercing it like a lance, and pieces of the worm shot out from its body. The thick pieces of meat hit the sand, shriveled up, and then vanished.

The exposed part of the worm toppled over on the opposite side of where Cory was, burned and torn to pieces, barely recognizable as the monster that had first surfaced.

Cory felt his lungs give out, and his screaming stopped.

He fell forward, and the fall hurt, but as he lay on the sand, it coddled him in soft arms.

"You happy, Larry? You happy, you big old bully," he said, and went to sleep.

*

The orange liquid poured onto his chubby face. His eyelids twitched twice, and then opened.

Cory sat up, and looked around. He was back in Old Man Gunther's basement, but for some reason, it reeked like citrus.

Larry stepped closer to him and kneeled down. "Hey man, you feeling okay?"

Cory touched the liquid that was running down through his hair and down his face. It was cold and sticky. He looked at it, and saw it was orange. "What the hell?"

Larry turned to Sheila to give her a chastising look. She held the can the soda had come from in her hand, and shrugged. "Sheila poured that to wake you up."

"Soda? You couldn't have used water?" Cory got up, and Larry followed.

They were all standing in a circle now, and despite his head being sticky, Cory was glad to see Stan wasn't bound to his chair anymore.

"I grabbed the first thing I saw," Sheila said. "Sorry, Core."

"You saved me," Stan said, and couldn't help but grin.

"Yeah, yeah," Cory said, "what? You want a hug or something?"

The truth was, Cory wanted to hug *all three of them* after that encounter with the Death Worm, but he wasn't about to look like a sissy.

"Not from you, fatty," Stanley said, and grinned at him.

Cory grinned back at him because he knew between the lines of the insult, Stan was thanking him the only way boys thanked one another while still trying to look cool and tough in front of others.

"How'd I get back?" Cory asked.

Larry shrugged. "You just kind of... appeared."

"Oh." He replied.

"Yeah," Larry said.

"We gonna go finish this stupid game, or what?" Cory asked, turning their attention back to the board behind them.

They all gulped.

Larry stepped away from them and stood over his chair, staring at the board. "Sheila, unless you get a crappy roll this turn, you're our best bet."

While he spoke, the other children took their seats. Stan and Cory were glad to see that the sand had vanished underneath their spots and the normal floorboard was there.

Sheila grabbed the die and scanned the board. If she rolled a 1, she'd land on a blank spot, a 2 would land her in the same spot as Cory, a 3 would be another blank spot, and then a 4 would put her in a red one. A 5 would put her in a blue spot, and if the previous turns were any indication, that would mean she'd get a good card. A 6 would put her in another blank spot.

She hoped for a 6 or a 5.

"Hold on," Larry said, "don't roll yet."

"Hm?" She said.

Larry turned to Cory. "You gonna tell us what happened when you got dragged into the sand, or what?"

Cory nodded. "I went into a room made of sand. Like a desert, except with walls. And then a giant worm with a huge mouth popped out of the ground."

Larry realized he had been holding his breath, and took in a deep one through his mouth. "Did you kill it?"

"Yeah," Cory shook his head, "I don't know what it was, but there was... a magical feeling inside of me, and I shouted and light came out and killed that thing."

"Whoa," Stanley said, "that's... awesome."

Cory looked at him and shook his head again. "Only awesome 'cause I lived through it. I was about ready to crap my pants."

He gestured his chin at the board. "We gotta burn this damn thing when we're done with it."

Larry nodded. "Yeah, man."

Unless... Cory's mind turned to another thought. Larry met his gaze, and he knew they were both thinking the same thing.

Unless if we try to burn it, the game will seek revenge against us.

That was later, they'd think about that after the now was complete.

"Come on Sheila, roll something good," Cory said.

Sheila let the die go. It rolled and came up a 5.

They all yelled out "yes!" as a group and high-fived one another, while the imp moved through the board to the blue spot.

Something happened when the imp reached the blue spot. It began to glow, emitting the same blue aura that the knight had when Cory was trapped in the sand room.

"Uh…" Stanley said, "what's going on?"

Sheila picked up the glowing blue card with the unicorn horn depicted on it off the ground. She had knocked it over when she ran around to pull Larry back after Cory got pulled by the sand, and they had all forgotten about it.

But the Board of Doom hadn't.

The imp continued until it hit the eighth spot from where it had been, and landed on a yellow spot.

The kids all looked at one another.

Red meant bad.

Blue meant good.

Yellow, they didn't know what to expect.

Sheila picked up a yellow card and read it. "*Game Event: The two-headed Beast of Doom has been summoned. Defeat the beast in 5 turns with a blue card, or the entire party meets its doom.*"

She put the card down. All of her friends were pale now.

"This game is ruthless," Larry said.

They didn't know what the two-headed beast was, but they knew one of them had to roll on to a blue spot.

Or…

"No! Screw that! I want to make her re-roll." Larry said, "Hey, game! Keeper, whatever, I'm using my wizard's ability to make Sheila re-roll that turn."

Cory grabbed his knees and squeezed. "Man, I hope it's not too late."

The die floated up into the air, then flew across the table and landed in front of Sheila. Larry gave her a reassuring look, and she picked it up and rerolled.

2, and with the Horn of the Unicorn card, that meant she actually rolled a 5. The imp moved back 3 spaces, and Sheila picked up the blue card from the deck.

"*Bow from the Heavens: Use this weapon to stop a red card.*"

"My dad told me about this kind of stuff," Cory said.

"What?" Stanley asked.

"Yeah, what're you talking about?" Larry said.

"He said 'the house always wins.' " Cory answered.

Larry leaned back in his chair and crossed his arms. The fright of the game and the victory of Cory beating the Death Worm had worn off. "What the hell are you babbling about now?"

" 'The house always wins,' you stupid ass. It's what they say in Vegas. My dad goes there on business trips, and I heard him tell his friends that his wedding ring always comes off when he goes there. That, and 'the house always wins.' "

"What does that mean?" Sheila asked.

"It means the casinos set the games up so that they always win."

"You're saying…" Larry stopped to consider it.

"The game gave me a blue card, but unless I figured it out, I would've been eaten by the Death Worm. Then it probably would've eaten Stan, too. And the game also gave Sheila a blue card, but now it forced you to use your wizard's reroll."

"You're right," Stan said, "and whatever she picks up from the blue pile, the game will force her to use it or it'll kill one of us."

"No matter what," Cory added, "bad stuff is going to keep happening to us."

"The odds are against us." Larry said.

"We'll have to work together to get through this," Cory said. "Everyone better pull their weight."

There was a fat joke in there, but none of them were in the mood to be humorous.

Besides, he was right. They'd have to play as a group to beat the Keeper of the Board, and all of his monstrosities.

*

Something happened when Larry picked up the die, something that none of them could have expected. To the others, it looked like their friend fainted while wearing a Halloween mask of a skeleton. A very real Halloween mask, because it didn't appear to be made of flimsy, cheap plastic. This was the real deal, made of bone. Made of someone or something's skull.

The mask attached itself to his face, and Larry saw nothing but blackness. He felt his head loll forward, then loll backward, and then his mind shut off.

"Oh crap, what's happening to him?" Cory said, ready to get up and shake him awake.

"The Mask of the Dead," Sheila reminded them, pointing at the red card glowing on Larry's side of the table. "He drew it last turn."

Cory crept over to Larry's chair, remembering whose voice it was that he heard when he had been trapped in the sand room. He poked him on the shoulder. "You think he can feel anything?"

"Uh, who knows?" Stan said.

Cory smirked, an idea suddenly forming.

He went back to his chair and rummaged through the front pocket of his book bag, and took out a pen that had been there since the last school year. Then he walked back to Larry, picked his right arm up and wrote I'M A DINGLEBERRY on the top of his hand.

Stan couldn't help but laugh. "You're *such* a jerk."

Cory giggled, and then went back to his chair. "I guess he wakes when I take my turn?"

From across the table, and with a smile, Sheila shrugged at the question.

He picked up the die and shrugged. "Guess we'll find out."

*

Pitch black. The space he was in was confined, too. Although he couldn't see where he was, couldn't even see the outline of his own nose if he tried, he could somehow feel that the walls of whatever he was trapped inside of were only centimeters away from him. If they were alive, he would feel them breathing down his neck.

Above him, also only centimeters away from his face, he could hear dirt being shoveled onto the top of the enclosure he was in. He realized what was happening; he was in a coffin, and he was being buried alive.

His heart and mind began to race.

He screamed, and punched at the lid of the coffin, but he knew it was useless. He knew he was trapped, knew he'd die in here.

These thoughts only made him scream louder.

*

Cory rolled a 5.

But with the knight's effect in play, it only moved four spaces across the board. Another blank spot.

"Been getting lucky here," Cory said, "I wonder when the Keeper will catch on to it and… I don't know, do something to make me regret it."

Just as he finished his sentence, Larry woke. The mask was off his face, and the memory of being buried alive was gone from his mind, but his heart raced and there was a brooding feeling somewhere in the back of his head. The feeling of waking up from a nightmare that felt all too real.

"How long was I out for?"

"Until my knight moved on the board," Cory said. "Why?"

He shook his head. "I don't know, I don't remember going to sleep. I just remember… actually, I don't really remember much. Except that I was experiencing something scary."

"Tough shit. Tell your mom to take you to a therapist once we kick this game's ass," Cory said, picking up the die to hand over to Stanley.

Larry rubbed the back of his neck, feeling even sillier for vocalizing it. He noticed the writing on the back of his hand. "Hey, what the heck?"

Cory laughed, and Stan and Sheila joined in with him.

Larry's face turned red, from both anger and embarrassment, and he kicked the table.

"Chill out," Sheila said, centering the table back in place, "it's just a stupid joke, Larry."

Larry shot daggers at Cory with his eyes, and Cory's grin grew bigger.

Stanley took the die to get the focus back to the game. He let it roll across the board. 3.

"Oh come on!" Stanley said, jumping to his feet in frustration.

He wasn't a sore loser, and didn't care too much about winning as long as he was having fun, but the stakes in this game were higher, the tension more pronounced.

The cowboy moved three spaces through the board, and landed on a yellow space. Stanley looked around at his friends before picking up a card, and they all nodded encouragement to him.

He read it to them: "*Cold was the night the living dead returned.*"

Sheila groaned.

The yellow card in Stanley's hand glowed, and a single snowflake danced its way down from the ceiling and landed on top of the brass cowboy's hat.

Then, the snow came down in a blizzard. Cold air rushed into the basement—but not from outside, no, outside it was the end of summer, a low of 60 degrees Fahrenheit, if that. The bitter cold came rushing in from somewhere else, from somewhere parallel to their world, perhaps.

All four of the kids hugged their chests and rubbed their arms with the opposite hands.

Through chattering teeth, Cory said, "W-w-well, this sucks."

"How do w-we, get rid of this?" Sheila asked.

Larry got out of his chair, but kept rubbing at his arms. There was a closet in the back of the basement with a door that was barely still on its hinges, but he remembered seeing old jackets in there that had belonged to Old Man Gunther. He was here by himself one summer when he ventured into that closet, and he remembered it smelling like mothballs, but there were at least two of them in there, and right now any extra layer of clothing would do.

"Wh-where are you g-going?" Stanley asked.

He was far too cold and miserable to waste energy at the moment. It would be better to show them. Once in front of the closet, he didn't bother to open it the regular way but instead barged through, shoulder first. The jackets were thrown across a wooden rack, forgotten and covered in dust. Larry grabbed them, and he heard them crunch in his hand. They smelled worse than he remembered, but that was okay. Only Cory would complain.

To his joy, there were two sweaters underneath the jackets, folded up and stuffed in the corner shelf of the rack, and he grabbed one of them and threw it over his head. It was brown and dark green, and he felt like Freddy Krueger, but it was better than turning into Jack Frost.

He left the closet and was rounding the wall back to the others when he almost bumped into Cory, who stopped when he saw him coming toward him.

"W-what—" Then he saw what was in Larry's hands and grabbed the top jacket out of the pile and threw it on. He sighed in satisfaction as the (itchy) wool almost immediately warmed him.

Even though he was a big kid, he was rounder than he was tall, and the jacket was way too big for him. He felt like a miniature version of his dad when he got summoned to jury duty, but he didn't care. It was better than freezing his ass off.

"Take it off, fatass," Larry instructed.

"What? Why? Screw you." Cory crossed his arms.

"Because, Stanley is skin and bones, and the other jacket is for Sheila."

"Then what am I going to wear?"

"There's a sweater at the bottom of this pile," Larry said.

"Only nerds and geeks who eat their boogers wear sweaters."

Larry wanted to kick him, but it was too damn cold to be arguing with him. Instead, he marched past him and said, "Fine, do whatever you want."

Larry returned to where the two others were shivering and with halos of snow on their heads, and gave Sheila the jacket, and then threw the sweater over the table to Stanley. He slipped into it in a blur. The sweater wasn't very thick, but it was better than nothing.

Cory returned a few moments later and walked over to where Stanley was and took his jacket off. "Here, take the jacket, shrimp-boy, I'll wear the sweater."

Stanley looked up at him, thinking he was pulling some stupid gag on him. "You sure?"

Cory rolled his eyes and nodded. "Yeah, now take the jacket before I change my mind, poop-stain."

They exchanged clothing, and then Cory went back into his chair. He glowered at Larry and said, "You happy?"

"Glad to see you're growing up."

Cory gave him the finger, and then to Sheila said, "Alright, get something good. Better if you get something to stop this damn winter land."

"Let's hope so," she said. She always hated the cold, and wished she and her friends could move to Arizona, where she was from.

"These things smell like crap," Stanley blurted out.

Sheila took her turn and rolled a 3.

Two bad rolls from her in a row. It seemed her luck was beginning to run out.

The imp moved to a blank space.

"Better than turning the basement into a volcano or something," Larry muttered.

They could all agree on that, because now they were on their toes of what this board could do. It could transport them into other worlds, implant thoughts into their heads, and even change the weather conditions inside of the purple fog.

They truly were prisoners to the power of the Board of Doom until someone landed on the last spot.

"At least none of us are dead." His breath came out in a cloud as Cory said this.

Larry cupped his hands and blew on them to try to warm them up. It only helped a little. "Alright, my turn."

He picked the die off from the board and rolled. It came up 6, which meant the wizard would be landing on a yellow space.

Another event card. *Great.* He thought.

"Spoke too soon," Cory added.

"Yeah," Larry said, then picked up the yellow card. He cleared his throat and read it to the group, "*When the sun sets and the darkness comes out to play, the game continues.*"

As the last words uttered out of Larry, the lights in the basement flickered, and then went out, leaving them in total darkness.

Cory, or maybe it was Sheila, gasped.

The board and all of the pieces of the game, including the brass figures, glowed red. Like everything was made of glow-in-the-dark material, except they knew that wasn't what it was, it was the game's magic.

All four of them dragged their chairs closer to the coffee table to be in the light. It shone a ghastly reflection on all of their faces, making them look ghoulish.

It wasn't a campfire that was warming them up, but it was better than being in the dark and cold. At least the game showed that much mercy.

"Things just get worse and worse," Stanley said.

"Good thing is," Sheila said, and pointed to where Cory's knight currently stood, "is that the game is almost over. Cory can use his knight's ability to reach the top of the castle."

Cory looked around the board to see if they were all with the plan. They were. It was in their eyes.

His stomach grumbled, and he expected a fat joke, but it never came. In the cold, dark, mothball-smelling circle they formed around this eerie board, all humor was lost. All they wanted was to roll the die one last time and go home.

Eat some pork chops and macaroni & cheese, maybe. Cory thought.

"I'm using my knight's dice rolls!" He stuck his neck out into the air as far as it would go and shouted. He wanted to make sure whatever was out there heard him that the game would end this turn. "You hear that Keeper? You hear that with your stupid face?"

Larry gulped. They didn't know how far the "house" could rig the game with its powers.

Maybe because of Cory's taunting it would make him roll all 1s after using the knight's abilities, then they'd really be screwed. He wanted to tell him to shut up, but he couldn't bring himself to do it because Cory was the one pulling the team throughout the game so far.

The wizard was far behind Cory's knight, and it would take some serious bad luck on Cory's end and some serious good luck on his own end to catch up and win for them.

But I want to win. No way do I want that fatso to win.

The Mask of the Dead was off of his face, but he could feel it still pulling at his thoughts, as if it were massaging his brain with its dark fingers, molding unwanted thoughts into his mind.

He didn't like it. He didn't like it one bit.

Trying to brush these thoughts out of his mind, he grabbed the die and put it on Cory's side of the table.

"Win it for all of us, Core," he said, but felt envy tug at his heart.

"Don't worry four-eyes, I will," Cory responded, cupping the die into his chubby hand. "I roll it three times, I guess, and then it'll add up. If I roll over 8 on these three rolls, we win the game."

You win the game. Larry thought.

Cory looked at him as the thought flared in his mind, and what he saw in Larry's eyes made him wince back.

"What?" Larry said.

Cory shook his head. Must have been the lack of light and the game's creepiness making him see things. "Nothing. I'm gonna roll now."

"Do it already," Sheila said.

"Yeah, I'm ready to get the heck out of here," Stanley added.

Cory rolled, the die tumbled across the board and stopped inches before rolling off the table on Sheila's side. 4.

"Halfway there," Cory announced.

"Yeah," Stan said.

Sheila handed the die to Cory over the table, and he shook it in his closed hand and let it roll. 1.

"OH! Screw this!" Cory slammed his fist on the table so hard the die shifted. "This game is bullcrap."

"Cool your jets. Just roll again," Larry told him. He felt command of the group coming back to him.

Please roll two 1's, please, please. Larry shook his head to try to rid himself of the thoughts, and Sheila saw him doing it out the corner of her eye. It reminded her of when she'd accidently leave their dog Trotter out in the rain when mom and dad weren't home, he'd shake his head in the middle of the living room, sprinkling water all over the sofas.

"Larry?" She said.

"What?"

They were all looking at him now. The way they had been looking at Stanley when he had been caught in the sand.

"You alright?" Stan asked.

Larry nodded. "The game, it's... I don't know. Putting thoughts in my head."

"I'm going to roll." Cory interrupted.

Stan and Sheila diverted their attention to him, but kept a wary eye on Larry.

"I'm fine," Larry told them, hoping it would be true soon.

1, 1, 1, please come up a 1. No. Yes. No.

The die rolls totaled to 5, but with the knight's effect in play it would only move 4 spaces ahead. That meant that Cory had to roll a 4 or higher to win the game.

He kissed the knuckles of the hand holding the die. "Come on, come on, daddy needs a new pair of shoes."

"Daddy?" Stan said.

Cory shot him an evil glare, then let the die roll.

All of their hearts stopped as the plastic die tumbled across the table, over the Board of Doom, hit the brass knight on its way, then bounced backward.

5.

"YES!" Cory jumped out of his seat and chopped the sides of his thighs while thrusting his hips forward, the universal sign for *suck-it*. "Take that Keeper, you jerk-face!"

Stan leapt up into the air and gave Cory a big hug. "Yes! Yes! Yes! We did it!"

Sheila ran around the table to join them, and now it turned into a big group hug. She turned to Larry, who felt weighted down by the dark thoughts in his mind, anchored by jealousy, and forced a smile.

"Come on, Larry, come on! We did it!" she said, gesturing for him to join them.

Larry got up and hugged them as well, but there was something keeping him from really feeling any comradery in the embrace. Like there was a wall, invisible perhaps, between him and his friends.

Friends? His mind hissed at him. *They like Cory better.*

No they don't.

Oh yes they do, look at how he's the center of this group hug, and you're on the outskirts.

Shut up.

Make me! You can't, because I'm inside of you. I AM you. And I'm telling you, these are not your friends anymore. They're his *friends. Do you want to win them back?*

Yes.

Good. Then close your eyes, and let the darkness consume you.

Larry did as he was told. The warmth of his friends disappeared before him, and was replaced by a coldness he never experienced. It wasn't the cold of winter, but the cold of something else. A cold that didn't actually exist anywhere except in the dark crevices of his heart.

He opened his eyes, and all around him was the purple fog. The Keeper stood before him, his skeleton face twisted into a big grin.

"Welcome to the last phase of the game, Larry."

There was something on his face. He could feel the weight of it and see the outline of whatever it was from his peripheral vision. *The Mask of the Dead.*

"Bingo," the Keeper said.

"You can... read my mind?"

"Read your mind? Oh child, we are one now."

"What?"

The skull nodded. "That's correct, I am the Keeper, you are the Emissary, but together we are the Board of Doom. The only way out of this is to defeat your friend Cory when he reaches the top of Castle Light. If he defeats you, you die. If you defeat him, he dies, and you are the winner of the game."

Larry opened his mouth, unbelieving. "What? I didn't agree to this!"

"Oh, of course you did, child. And there's no takesy-backsy's in the game, so get yourself ready to fight for your life."

The fog to the right of the Keeper began to open up like a gate and reveal the entrance of a stadium. Even from here Larry could see every seat in the stands was occupied, and he could hear the crowd roaring.

"Don't look so frightened, child, I will be there to help you with all of my powers. Together, we will win the game and keep the order of the universe right. Understood?"

Larry nodded before he knew he was doing it.

He felt the cold slip away and be replaced with warmth again. Not good warmth, though, a hot and muggy warmth that seemed to choke him, even more so with the mask on his face.

He looked down at his body and saw he was wearing an onyx-colored suit of armor. It looked heavy and clunky, but he didn't feel any heavier. No, if anything, he felt lighter.

More aware, more powerful.

This was the power of the Board of Doom, this was true darkness. And he had to admit, it felt good.

"Now, let's take the game back, and take your friends back from him, shall we?"

"Let's do it," Larry said, and walked through the fog and into the stadium.

Part III: Endgame

He was huffing and puffing by the time he ascended the stairs and was on the castle's rooftop. He was overweight by at least 30 lbs., and any physical exertion always reminded him of this fact.

Matters were only made worse by the clunky suit of armor that he was wearing. No longer was he in Old Man Gunther's basement; heck, no longer was he in his hometown. He was somewhere extraordinary, somewhere that probably didn't even exist in the same universe.

At the top of the stairs, two giant wooden doors awaited him. They were the kind seen at the entrance of the renfair he and his dad attended every two years or so, only these were the real deal. The sword and shield hanging on each of the giant doors weren't decorations, but actual weapons that could be used on a battlefield.

"Wow," Cory said.

He felt like a hero, like someone who was accomplishing much more than just beating out some stupid game. He felt on top of the world.

With this confidence brimming inside of him as brightly as the suit of armor he was wearing shone, he pushed open the double doors.

The crowd broke into applause as the knight stepped into the arena, and Cory couldn't believe it. After years and years of trying to gain approval of his peers, here was an entire coliseum full of people applauding for *him*.

The hero. The winner. They weren't chanting his name, but he closed his eyes and imagined they were for a few seconds.

When he opened them, a set of double doors, similar to the ones he had gone through, opened on the opposite side of the stadium. A king with his royal family and royal entourage came through it. There were other knights in suits of armor like his own, and a queen with a red dress that floated behind her like an aura, and then a princess with a smile that was too beautiful to be real.

In fact, all of the royal family appeared too jovial to be real. If you touched them, you'd feel flesh, but the expressions on their faces were plastic-like.

A red carpet appeared between them when Cory wasn't looking, and his legs moved underneath him as if he were on a treadmill. At the same time, the king broke from the royal family and approached him. He moved rigidly, almost like an animatronic robot.

"Sir Knight," the king said, approaching him, "I am the King of the Board. I see you have ascended the top of Castle Light."

Cory bowed down on one knee. "Yes sir, I have conquered the Board of Doom, and now I ask that you end the game."

Just like his legs had been, his lips seemed to be running on a script.

The light shining down on the rooftop was swallowed up and replaced by darkness. Cory stood up out of his bow and saw the King continuing to smile, as if he were unaware of the sudden change in lighting.

Then, the force that had changed it made sure he and everyone else knew. A bolt of lightning came crashing down between Cory and the King.

The impact of the strike sent the King reeling backward, into the arms of two imperial guards that moved quickly to make sure the King didn't fall over.

The expression of cartoonish happiness on the royal family was replaced by cartoonish panic and bewilderment.

Cory wasn't thrown back by the force, but he did cover his face, take a few steps back and feel the heat of the lightning hit his armor.

The lightning stopped, and it left more than just a burn on the red carpet. A dark figure had emerged, as if it had ridden the lightning down from the dark sky to Castle Light's rooftop.

Cory put his arms down and saw the figure standing before him. It wore the Mask of the Dead that had knocked Larry out back a few turns ago, and wielded a strange sword. The sword was a weapon, evidenced by the sharpened edge, but there was an eyeball on either side of the sword, suggesting it was also a living thing. It pulsed in the knight's hands, and Cory thought he could hear the beat of the heart or whatever it was that kept that thing alive.

The Emissary of Darkness.

The thought came to him just as the name of the Keeper of the Board had when he had stepped into the purple fog, and he knew it was the name of this new entity.

He also knew this entity was the game's final attempt to keep him from winning.

"You must be the Keeper's crony, huh?" Cory said. The shadow knight stared at him. "And I guess, you're his last chance to stop me from winning."

The shadow knight responded, but Cory couldn't hear.

*

"No, fatso, this is *my* last chance to stop you from winning. To stop you from taking my friends away from me," Larry said, but he knew Cory couldn't hear him.

He knew the words were lost behind the Mask of the Dead. Even so, it felt good to say.

Something had happened when he crossed from the Keeper's dominion into the top of Castle Light, and that something was what was driving Larry now. He accepted the darkness and the powers it bestowed upon him, they were one now.

And he planned on using what he had to stop Cory from triumphing. This wasn't their fistfights and arguments as kids.

One of them would die.

The other would be declared the winner of the Board of Doom.

Larry had never lost to Cory in any video game—not even that shitty pinball game at Bill's Laundromat. He didn't plan on losing his life to this jerk.

"Get ready, Core," Larry said, "because here I come, and I'm not holding back."

The sword of darkness pulsed in his hand like the heart of a sprinter. It was fueled from the darkness of Larry's heart, after all.

*

In Cory's hand now was his own sword. It was broad and rivaled the dark sword in sharpness.

"You think I'm going to let some stupid game beat me?" Cory held the sword in front of him, the way the characters in his video games and comic books did. "After all the crap the game put me and my friends through, it's going to have to try harder than to send some creep in a mask to stop me from winning."

Cory charged full force at the dark figure. Recklessly, with no consequences in mind.

Played right into my hands, fatboy.

Larry held up the sword and unleashed a streak of lightning at Cory. This one didn't come down from the sky; this one shot horizontally like an electrical charge, and went straight at Cory.

Cory tried to sidestep the attack, but he was too late. In one last-ditch effort, he tried to swat away the lightning, but the gesture was ineffective. The blast sent him reeling backward and took him off his feet.

First blood, creepo, but if you think——

The dark figure was up in the air and coming straight down at him, sword pointed to stab him. Cory rolled away and heard the sword strike the rooftop with a metallic clink.

The force of the missed blow put Larry off balance, and he had to stick his arms out to wave them to re-center his gravity. This gave Cory enough time to pop up to his feet and close the distance in on him.

He chopped Larry's legs out from underneath him with the broadsword and then went to cut his head off at the neck, but Larry parried the blow with his sword and deflected the attack.

The surprise of the deflection made Cory have to step backward to keep himself from stumbling to the ground, and this gave Larry the few seconds to scoot himself away and jump up to his feet.

One for one. Cory thought. *I don't have any fancy-shmancy lightning attacks like you, Creepo, but I'm fighting for something more important than this stupid game.*

Cory gripped his sword as tightly as he could, until his knuckles were turning white, and then charged at Larry again. *I'm fighting for my friends.*

When he was within attack range, Cory slashed the sword vertically. Larry held his own sword out horizontally to parry the attack yet again. Cory expected it this time, and at the last second changed the direction of his attack and turned it into a stab.

Larry saw the change in the attack, from an arc to a lunging motion, and tried to act accordingly, but he was too late. The sword pierced through his arm, and then he felt the heatwave in his gut as the sword pierced through there, too.

Cory felt the armor break, then felt the tip of the sword break through flesh, and he knew he had it in the bag. He drove the sword forward, as hard as he could. The sword broke the armor on the other side of the dark figure's body.

The Mask of the Dead went flying off of the figure's face, out into the sky in a physically impossible way, and then the mask was obliterated into hundreds of pieces before winking out of existence—the dark magic that had created it losing all of its power.

Now Cory could see the figure's face. His fingers went numb, his whole arm went numb, and he felt revulsion in his stomach as he saw his friend's face twist into agony. The sword of darkness slipped out from his weakening grip and clattered to the ground.

Blood poured down from Larry's mouth in a flow of crimson, and then he bent forward. He would've fallen if not for Cory holding him up with the sword.

"Larry?" Cory said, but it wasn't his voice. It was the voice of a chump, the voice of a person as small as a thimble.

He let the sword go, and when he did so Larry and the weapon he had used to kill him lurched forward and crashed to the ground.

Cory fell to his knees and grabbed Larry's body. The hole where the sword had gone through was filled with blood and spilling over the armor.

"Larry? Larry?" Cory couldn't believe it.

It was an illusion. An illusion from the Keeper, one last trick to make him feel doomed, that had to be it. There was no way he had just killed his best friend, no damn way.

Larry's body, and the sword with it, disappeared into nothingness.

Just an illusion. Just a damn illusion from this damn game, he told himself, but he wasn't sure if he believed it.

*

The darkness in the sky went away, and the light returned, shining down like a beam from the heavens. It gave everything a beautiful radiance.

It didn't help to make Cory feel better, though, because there was still a shadow on his heart that weighed it down like an anchor. He was kneeling from when he had been holding Larry's body, and the shadow of someone standing over him cast down on him.

It was the King, and he was smiling the plastic smile again. This time he held something wrapped in a gold blanket, it looked big and tall, and Cory only had an inkling of what it was.

Cory stood up. The royal family and the royal entourage stood behind the King, all holding the same expression on their face they had when they first appeared through the double doors, as if nothing had happened between then and now.

No, because to them this was just a part of the script. They weren't real. Neither was the Larry he killed. This was all fake, all an illusion from the trickery of the stupid Board of Doom.

"Well done, Sir Knight, you have vanquished the Keeper's final ally, and have freed Castle Light from the clutches of the Board of Doom." He took the blanket off and it vanished into thin air as if it were mist to reveal a trophy with a ribbon tied to it. On the base of the trophy was etched the word "WINNER."

The King handed the trophy to Cory. He took it, and at the same time somewhere in the distance fireworks went off. Confetti fell from the sky through some magic. The crowd applauded, their clapping thunderous and even louder than the fireworks going off above the stadium.

A part of him wanted to soak it all in, because for the first time he was a winner. It said so on his trophy, it said so in the feeling he had seeing the crowd of people looking at him and clapping for him, but in his mind, he knew this was just the sweet side of a bittersweet moment.

He took one last look at the crowd, holding the trophy up over his head and moving in a circle so that all of his adoring fans could see his prize possession, and the next moment it all winked out of existence and he saw nothing but whiteness.

*

Then he was back in Old Man Gunther's basement. It wasn't cold, or dark anymore, everything was back to normal—sort of. He was on all fours and panting like a tired dog.

Stan put his hand on his back. "Hey, come on, Core. Get up."

Cory did, and although his legs felt rubbery, he was able to stand. He stood between Sheila and Stan, and both of them put a hand on each of his shoulders.

"It's over," Sheila said.

But where's Larry?

He scanned the room. The Board of Doom game was in the middle of the coffee table, packed up and ready to go back to the factory if need be (or to be burned). Sheila's empty soda can was the only other thing on the table, and even the bendy straw sticking out of it looked relieved that this was all over. The sweaters and coats that they had been using to keep warm from the stupid game's cold weather were thrown across a chair.

"The lights came on like thirty seconds ago, and the cold went away then, too," Sheila informed him.

"Where's Larry?" Cory asked.

Sheila shook her head. Stan did too.

Cory broke away from them and grabbed the game with both hands, ready to slam it against the table.

"Core, stop!" Sheila shouted. "Stop!"

He did and turned to face her. "I'm going to break this stupid fucking game if it's the last thing I do. I hate it!"

Sheila stepped closer to him and held her hands out, as if a cop dealing with a hostage situation, "Cory, listen to me. We know what that evil game can do, if you try to do something to it after the game is over, you might anger the Keeper."

"Keeper? I beat him already, I beat the damn game. I'm the master of the Board now, you hear me, Sheila? You hear me, Keeper? Me, me, me, I'm the winner."

Sheila and Stan looked at one another and both shrugged, but before either of them could do or say anything more, Larry appeared before them out of thin air.

Cory threw the game back on the table and ran over to his side. Larry was lying on his stomach, and Cory flipped him onto his back. It wasn't until he saw the blood running out of his mouth that he also felt the blood on his own fingers.

It was hot and sticky, and sent terror through his heart.

The Larry on top of Castle Light had been the real Larry, and the wound from his sword had been real, too. It gushed out blood in every direction. Little rivulets of red ran down from his stomach to the floor.

Cory smacked him across the face, but that did nothing except throw a spray of blood up Cory's arm, so he started punching him in the chest.

"Get up, idiot. Stop messing around, get up, Larry. Get up."

Sheila and Stan were too confused and too shocked to move, so they watched instead.

Cory punched him harder and harder, until his hand started to lose feeling. Then he clutched his shirt and put his forehead on Larry's still body, and cried. "Get up, get up, get up whiz kid. Who the hell is going to call me a butt-munch when I'm acting like an idiot if you're dead? Huh? Huh? Get up, get up, please. Please. I'm sorry, man. You win, you win, the trophy is yours."

He began to hyperventilate, and hoped this was Larry getting him back for all the years of bullying and lying, and he'd slap him in the back of the neck and get up. He'd be pissed, he'd want to kick his ass, but it'd be better than this.

Anything would be better than this.

A few minutes went by, and Larry didn't move.

His friend was dead, and he was the one who had killed him.

*

The kids told everyone that they had been hanging out at Old Man Gunther's house and all of them except Larry decided to go play down in Bunker Woods. Larry decided to stay back to read comic books until dinner time. When they came back, they found him dead in the middle of the basement.

The police had no other choice but to call it murder. There had been reports of drug addicts in surrounding suburbs—not any in their town until Larry was "murdered" by one—but the connection was there.

A drug addict tried to break into Old Man Gunther's abandoned house, saw a boy was there, got scared and stabbed him. Made more sense than a haunted board game, after all.

Larry's funeral was a week after his death, and the three children avoided one another even at school. It was awkward and strange, but all three of them felt like being too close to the others would bring back the evil of the game somehow, so they just stayed away.

Even Stan and Sheila didn't talk. And Stanley would only nod to Cory if they passed in the hallway, and that was that.

They hung out with other kids in their class, but if one of them was in a group at recess or at a lunch table, they'd avoid that group and go play or sit with another group. Their school wasn't very big, but people broke up into different cliques so there were enough groups for their separation. Eventually Stan, Cory, and Sheila each settled into one group that had no association with the other one, and everything ran smoothly.

At the funeral, they only said hello, gave each other a hug, and cried on each other's shoulders. The only other words that were exchanged were from a note that Cory slipped into Stan's jacket pocket when they hugged in the middle of the cemetery.

Stan found the crumpled piece of paper in his jacket on the car ride home, at first thinking it was a receipt from his weekend trip with his cousin to Doughnutville, but when he opened it up, Cory's chicken-scratch was unmistakable. It read:

Meet me in front of Old Man Gunther's @ 8:30. Sheila too.

Under his breath, he asked himself, "Sheila, too? What the heck is that supposed to mean?"

He tried to think like Cory for a second, and decided he was trying to tell him to tell Sheila to come with him.

So later that night he called her, and to his surprise, she answered the phone. On the first ring, at that. It was almost as if she had been waiting by the phone for him to call the whole week.

"Hello?" She said. Her voice was croaky, and he imagined she had been crying.

"Hey, Sheila, it's Stan." He wanted to ask her if she remembered him. It felt like a lifetime ago that all four of them had been shooting the shit in Old Man Gunther's basement and giving Cory a hard time.

"Hey, Stanley, how are you?"

"Fine. You?"

"Fine, too, I guess."

Stanley cleared his throat. "Core wants to get the old gang back together."

The old gang, minus Larry. Because he's—well, you know, were the unspoken words trapped behind his lips.

"What? When?"

"Tonight, in front of Old Man Gunther's. He left me a note in my jacket."

Sheila giggled. It came off unsure and strange, as if she hadn't been sure she could still produce that noise until she tried just now. "That's so, jeez, that's so Cory-like."

"Yeah," Stan said, and grinned. It was.

Maybe this was a sign of things to come. "So, what do you think, Sheila? You gonna come?"

"I'll have to sneak out of the house. My parents don't want me out after dark ever since what happened to Larry," she told him.

"Yeah, that makes sense," Stan said, and looked up at the clock. "The note said 8:30. Which gives us about half an hour to go meet up with him."

"I'll start planning my escape now then," Sheila said and laughed again, "see you then, Stan."

"Yeah, see ya then Sheila," Stan said, and put the phone back on the receiver.

He didn't have the same issue with his parents, he wouldn't have to sneak out, but he'd need a damn good excuse to leave the house at that hour if his parents were going to say yes. He went out the back door, seeing his parents in front of the glow of the TV on his way out, and went to the shed where his bike was.

He'd take a screwdriver to his tire, tell them it happened on his way home from school and he was going to get it fixed really quick so he didn't have to walk to school tomorrow.

*

Cory sat on the porch of Old Man Gunther's house, chewing on the nail of his thumb. It was the second week of September, and it got chilly at this hour of the night, so he wore a thin jacket that blew in the wind and flapped like a flag. It was annoying him.

But even more annoying were the bugs that were still out, buzzing by his head. They seemed to be taunting him, telling him that his friends weren't coming because they knew he was the one who murdered Larry. That, plus they were scared of the black magic that came out of the stupid game.

The game was by his feet, and he kicked it. Inside he heard all of the pieces—the brass figures, the cards, the die—shift.

He stuck his hands in either pocket of his jacket, where he had a can of lighter fluid in one and a box of matches in the other. If Stan and Sheila didn't show in fifteen minutes, he'd torch the fucking thing himself and go home and call it a night.

He'd have a hard time coming to terms with losing two of his best friends—no, losing *all three* of his best friends, but he supposed he'd get over it. Things could have been worse; the three of them could have lost their lives that day they played the Board of Doom, as well.

But these thoughts dispersed the moment he heard the murmur of conversation coming up the hill, followed by the sound of a floppy tire slamming against the pavement leading to Old Man Gunther's driveway.

Cory jumped up, and saw both Stan and Sheila were walking up the hill to meet him. A second ago, he thought Stanley wouldn't even show up, and now here they both were. He felt tears coming up to his eyes and wiped at them with the back of his hand.

"Stan! Sheila! Yo!" He said, and waved to them.

They waved back, and in that instant of greeting one another, it was how it always had been, how it was always supposed to be, back when Larry was still alive.

Stan and Sheila stopped at the top of the hill and Stan put the kickstand down on his bike, then they walked the rest of the way to where Cory was waiting for them.

Their smiles wavered for a second when they saw the Board of Doom behind him.

Cory saw their concern and tried to deflect their attention. "What's up with the bike?"

Stan shrugged. "I had to find an excuse my parents would buy to get out of the house."

Sheila rolled up her pant leg and showed Cory a series of scratches from the thorny bush at the bottom of her bedroom window. "And I sacrificed my precious legs for this, so this better be good, Core."

The cheerfulness and happiness went out of him, making him feel even more deflated than Stanley's bike tire. He walked over to the porch, and they followed behind him but remained standing when he sat on the steps.

"I have something to tell you guys," he said, and felt tears building up in his eyes again. "It'll probably make you hate me, if you don't already, but oh well. I have to tell you guys, all things considered."

"What is it?" Sheila asked. "Does it have to do with—"

"Larry's death, yeah," Cory said. "When I got to the top of Castle Light, I had to face the Emissary of Darkness, and I didn't know it until it was too late, but that was Larry. He was still wearing the Mask of the Dead—remember?"

They did remember, but the feelings and experience felt so far in the distance that it may as well have been a nightmare they all had shared one night. Of course, it had been real, and the only proof they needed of that was the box sitting by their feet and their dead friend, but even still, hearing Cory talk about these events was like listening to someone talk about a time that no longer existed.

"Yeah," Stanley said.

"I'm the one who stabbed him. I'm the one who killed him." He looked down at his feet, at his worn Chuck Taylors, and expected he'd cry. When he thought about finally telling them the truth, he always envisioned himself crying like a baby, but now that he told them, he didn't.

In fact, he felt better about it all. Not *good*, but better now that the truth was out, no matter how much they suspected that he had been the one who killed Larry, now they *knew* what happened, and that made him feel better.

Even if it meant they'd hate him.

Stanley sat down next to him, and the old steps creaked underneath even his insignificant weight. He put his arm around him, and said, "Don't blame yourself, Cory. It's not your fault, it's the stupid game's fault."

Cory nodded. "You really think so?"

Sheila sat on the other side of him and now she had her arm around him as well. "We know so, Core. The game pitted us against each other, even though it gave us the illusion that we were working together."

"Yeah," Cory said, and now felt the sting in his eyes from tears welling up.

"You might not forgive yourself at this very moment, Core, but you will eventually," Sheila said. "We can't undo what we did that day in that basement, but it's no use to beat yourself up over this."

Cory met her eyes, and saw she meant every word of it. She wasn't just saying this to make him feel better the way his mom told him he'd lose his belly when he hit his teen years. He took the lighter fluid and matches out of his jacket and showed them to her.

"Do you think I should burn it?" Cory asked.

To his surprise, she shook her head. "No, we don't know what that will do. I think we should take it into Bunker Woods, deep in the woods, and bury it so no one can ever find it."

"Yeah, I agree." Stanley said, then clapped Cory on the back. "And I second what Sheila said. You need to forgive yourself about this whole thing. It could've been any of us that killed Larry, or that could've been dead. That day wasn't any of our faults except for the part where we decided to play the game. That's it."

Cory put the matches and lighter fluid away and smiled weakly. This was why he considered them his best friends, and why the week they had been apart felt so long and agonizing, and it felt great that they were back together. "Man, I thought I'd never say this, but I missed you guys."

Stanley and Sheila exchanged looks, and then both got up and started back to Stanley's bike. Cory got up, smiling and in high spirits.

"So after we bury the game tomorrow, we'll hang out again, right guys?"

Once again the two looked at one another, and Sheila stepped forward and patted his shoulder.

"Stan and I agree that it's best we all go our separate ways, out of respect for Larry. He was, after all, the reason we were all friends, and it just wouldn't feel right for us to hang out without him, you know?"

"What? No, no! Larry would want us to, want us to—"

Sheila put a thin finger up to his lips. It was cold and smelled like cotton candy. "We can be nice to each other, okay? But we can't hang out together anymore, this whole thing is tainted. You have other friends now, and so do I and Stanley. It's best we start over with them and try to forget about this, okay?"

The only feeling that rivaled this feeling of heartbreak was when he saw Larry was dead. He felt crushed, he felt small, he felt like melting and disappearing through the cracks in the sidewalk. He couldn't believe it, but another part of him knew she was right.

Larry had been the glue that had held them together; without him here, they wouldn't know what to do. Without his guidance, they'd just be sitting around yelling at one another and would eventually grow to hate each other. It'd be better this way, he knew it, deep in his heart he knew it'd be better if they just stayed distant acquaintances rather than try to force a friendship.

But knowing that didn't make it any easier, and it sure as hell didn't make it any less hurtful.

Cory watched his old best friends go down the hill back into town. They weren't talking, and the only sound besides the crickets in the grass was the thumping of Stanley's floppy bike tire hitting the pavement.

Sheila stopped when they were almost too small to see anymore, and saw him staring down at them. She put her hand up and waved to him, and Cory waved back.

He couldn't believe it. He had gotten all of the die rolls right, had used the cards he was drawn at the right moment, had triumphed against the Board. The King had given him the trophy proclaiming him The Winner, but still he lost.

He killed his best friend.

Lost his two other best friends, because...

Because, *the house always wins.*

RODENT GOD

The smell of them in your nose, the reflection of them in your eyes, the warmth of their skin underneath your touch. When your significant other is around you, chemicals in your brain react to produce love. It's a beautiful thing.

Some would say that it's destiny, a pairing of two souls that were meant for each other finally coming together and fitting like two pieces of a jigsaw puzzle.

No matter how it's described, it can be agreed that the other side of it is awful. Even if you've never experienced it yourself, the thought of falling in love with someone and then having it ripped away from you is mortifying.

A broken heart seems to have no mend. It seems like it will bleed for an eternity. It hurts somewhere that isn't palpable or concrete, and that's what makes it so much worse. It ruins a part of the person that was made whole by the other, the one who broke it in the first place.

And sometimes, a broken heart leads people to do things they will regret. Sometimes, the heartbreak drives the person crazier than the actual love ever could have.

*

Marcy had called him fifteen minutes ago in the middle of his lunchbreak, which was funny because he had planned on calling her first to tell her that he won tickets to go see Showrun—her favorite local band—from some radio contest that morning. But instead she beat him to the punch, and then punched his heart out.

With each word, he had felt his heart ache worse and worse. When he was in high school, he worked at a pretzel shop one summer, and he imagined his heart as the dough he used to twist and bend into the shape of the mallrats' favorite snack.

It's not you, it's me. I need some time to myself. I need some time to think, she had said.

With each uninvited twist, he imagined his heart ejecting his soul out in the form of blood.

It hurt like hell. It hurt like nothing he had ever experienced.

Now, Walter sat cross-legged on the floor behind a stairwell. It was a low traffic area of the building, even during lunch hours. Which left him just with his thoughts and a mousetrap smeared with peanut butter that Ernesto, the janitor, had set up in the darkest corner.

There were mice in every building, but there was something off-putting about the mousetrap being underneath a stairwell that led right into a lunch room.

On another day, he would have sat on these thoughts and been more disturbed by it, but the weight of the break-up was threatening to crush him.

He couldn't believe it. He was blindsided. There had been no signs that Marcy had been unhappy. Shit, just last week they had gone to her nephew's birthday party and picked out his Monsters Inc. action figures together.

Who could have known as they walked down the aisles laughing and joking about the toys they used to play with when they were children, that somewhere deep in her heart she was concocting a plan to break it off, to break *him*.

He was hurt and distraught, but didn't feel like crying at the moment. There was something holding him back, something keeping him from the reality of the situation, but he knew once it set in that he'd be crushed and feel even shittier.

While these thoughts rifled through his mind like a deck of cards on a casino table, a small mouse crawled out of the opposite corner of where the mousetrap was. For whatever reason, an uninvited rodent's appearance always froze people in their tracks, and this one's magic worked even on him.

He stopped thinking about Marcy and watched the mouse's whiskers flick the air, smelling the food several feet away.

Then the misery returned, and he thought that if he were the size of the mouse, he would end it by letting the trap decapitate him.

The mouse inched forward. The staircase was so quiet Walter could hear its little pink feet clicking on the marble floor. It stopped at the edge of the mousetrap and sniffed. It smelled the food better than ever now, but it also smelled the danger.

You could end it all. If you have any troubles, little mouse—maybe there isn't enough food in the building. Maybe you go to bed with a grumbling stomach every night. You could end it. Just stick your head in the trap and it'll all be over...

The mouse stuck its neck out, mouth open to bite the peanut butter, and then *SNAP!*

The metal bar clamped down on its neck and broke it in the blink of an eye. Walter stared at the dead body in some horror, because he hadn't thought the mouse was going to fall for it. He had been sure of it—somehow—that the mouse had smelled the danger hovering over the smell of the food and was going to get away safely.

It was almost as if his thoughts had willed it, as if...

The watch on his wrist beeped that lunch was over, and he got up. He took one last glance over at the mouse; its head was mostly separated from its body, only attached by a string of veins or tissue or something. He couldn't really see underneath the coating of blood.

He felt like he should clean it up, like it was his responsibility somehow, but then the thought went away and he got out from underneath the staircase and headed back to the office.

*

He was prepared to wake up every hour even if his mind found a way to shut itself off that night, but what he wasn't prepared for was for the mice in the walls to be scratching all night. They scratched, and scratched, and scratched, until he couldn't take it anymore.

It was a one-two punch of insomnia, not only was his mind restless with thoughts of what he could have done differently to save his relationship with Marcy, how he could have been a better boyfriend, but the mice wouldn't fucking stop. It was like they were having an orgy all night long, and hundreds of them had been invited.

He lay in his bed, looking up at the ceiling while the mice scratched away. He balled his hand into a fist and punched the wall. The framed Jimi Hendrix poster hanging by his bed fell to the ground.

The mice stopped.

Walter rolled over on his stomach and closed his eyes.

A few seconds later, the scratching started up again.

He turned to his back again and opened his eyes.

"Give me a fucking break here!" He yelled, not caring if his neighbors heard.

But it didn't work, they continued scratching, and actually his yelling had made it worse because now he could hear them scurrying through the tunnels in his wall, as if riled up.

Wanting to bash his head through the wall, he got up and went to the kitchen to grab a beer.

The fridge was stocked with Heineken for the first time since he had been dating Marcy. She didn't like him drinking during the week and accused him of doing it when he had his fridge stocked, so to avoid a fight he just quit drinking altogether while he was with her.

He grabbed a beer, it was cold and felt good in his hands, and would feel even better going down his throat. He sat down at his breakfast table and cracked it open with a corner—an old trick he used to use back in his college days to impress freshman girls at parties.

The bottle cap fell to the floor, bounced and went between the breakfast table's back leg and the wall. This was a testament to how long it had been since he'd done the trick; in his heyday, he had always been fast enough to catch it.

For a second, he thought of bending down to get it, thinking that Marcy would be mad if he forgot about it and she found it the next time she came over.

Then he realized that there wouldn't be a next time.

He put the bottle to his lips and let the beer rush into his mouth. It was crisp, cool, and exactly what he needed. He drank most of it in that single gulp, and though he didn't have plans to get wasted on a work night, he was already thinking of grabbing another when this one was finished.

It wasn't until swig three that he noticed the sound behind him. The mice were scratching in this room, as well. It was as if the mice had followed him. Or better yet, as if he had led them here.

He set the beer down with some vigor and swung out of the stool. He crossed the kitchen to the wall where the mice were and crossed his arms in front of his chest. *Okay guys, tell me what the hell is up your asses tonight.*

They seemingly responded to his thoughts, because the mice broke out into a chorus of squeaks. With each squeak, their message came through louder and clearer to Walter.

We want to help…

The murmur turned into a message that was blasting through his ears. He couldn't have ignored it even if he wanted to.

We want to help… help, help, help.

Walter put his hand against his temples, thinking he was going crazy, but the mice kept going. Insisting that they wanted to help him.

Help you, help you, help you.

"Fine!" Walter said, and looked to the closet in his living room where he kept the sledgehammer the maintenance man had left a few weeks ago. "You want to help? You want to help me? *Fine.*"

He marched through the living room, ripped the closet door open, and grabbed the sledgehammer. Then he returned to the kitchen, with the intentions of smashing each and every one of the mice that was behind the wall.

But once he broke through, he would have a different idea.

*

While Walter swung the sledgehammer at his kitchen walls and tried to decide if he was going crazy or not, across town Marcy slept. She kept tossing and turning all night, much to the chagrin of her cat Frankie, who'd wake up at every sudden movement. He'd let out a small growl, lick the small of his back, and then go back to sleep until the next disturbance.

It wasn't so much the guilt of breaking Walter's heart that kept her up, no that was a part of it, but not the worst part. The worst part was the thought that she might have made a mistake. That in a few months she'd get lonely and ask him to get back with her, but by then he might've moved on.

That was all paranoia; she knew that because he had once told her that this was his first "real" relationship—whatever that meant. There was no way Walter wouldn't take her back. He would if that's what she wanted.

But the reality didn't matter. What mattered was the doubt that kept slipping into her mind.

She sat up and turned the lamp on by her bedside. Frankie was on his back, his white belly exposed to her and his eyes half open. She rubbed his stomach, and he batted at the air and then closed his eyes.

The clock by her lamp read 4:15 am.

Two hours until she'd get up for her morning jog. Her throat felt dry, and a cold drink of water sounded good about now, so she swung out of bed and put on her slippers.

Frankie knew this meant she was going to open the door, so he jumped out of the bed. Yawning, he stretched his back out.

Then he followed her out of the room.

*

The wall was destroyed. Plaster and insulation hung out from the hole in the wall like guts. The kitchen wasn't very big so the dust had flown all over the place and covered the cabinets, stove, and refrigerator. If it weren't for the gigantic hole, someone walking in would've thought he had gone crazy while making pizza dough.

Walter felt crazy, but it had nothing to do with pizza and everything to do with the mice that had crawled out of the wall. There were a bunch of them, probably close to thirty but no more than forty, and they were lined up in front of his appliances as if in ranks. Their beady eyes all stared at him, their whiskers twitched.

Walter stared back at them from across the kitchen where he sat, and ran his hand through his hair. He was sweating from swinging the sledgehammer at the wall, sweating from the uncertainty of the situation.

"What do you want from me?" he asked the mice.

They're going to eat me, he thought.

One by one, the mice rose on their hind legs and squeaked. They did it at a coordinated tempo, so as to convey a message.

By the tenth squeak, Walter understood what they were saying, as if granted the knowledge of their language.

We are here to serve you, Master.

"What?" Walter ran his hand through his hair again, sure that he was crazy, sure that this was just one big nightmare.

His hand was clammy and cold with sweat. He rubbed his palm at the front of his pants.

The mice continued squeaking at him. *You're not going crazy, Master. This is your destiny, this is* our *destiny. To serve you in time of need.*

"To serve me? I don't understand." Walter said, sitting up.

Two of the mice faced each other, and squeaked. Then one of them ran across the kitchen floor into the next room. From this angle, Walter could see into the living room. The mouse went underneath his sofa, found a hole in the cloth, then used the inside structure of the furniture to climb to the top of it and pop out from a hole in the back of the headrests. Once on top of the couch, the mouse ran over to where Walter's keys were hanging on a nail hammered into a wooden plank by the front door.

Using its front paws, the mouse grabbed the keys and then, holding them in its mouth, went back into the hole it crawled out of. It climbed down the sofa, and returned into the kitchen. It set the keys by Walter's legs.

At first he didn't get it. They were just his regular house keys. There was the silver one for the apartment door, the long one with the Ford logo on the top, his soccer ball keychain, and the keychain that Marcy had gotten for him—

His eyes fell on the keychain he put on his ring a week ago, when Marcy had returned from her trip to Egypt. He picked up his keys by the center ring, and let them dangle in front of him.

The staff keychain was supposed to be a miniature replica of some Egyptian relic that allowed the pharaohs to control rats, or so she had told him.

He didn't think anything of it when she gave it to him, just another one of the many hunks of junk she always brought back on her trips for him, and he wouldn't have thought anything of it now if it weren't for the glowing gem on the end of it.

It glowed bright red, as if awake. He moved it away from the kitchen light to under the shadow of his thigh to make sure that it wasn't just a trick of the light.

It wasn't.

He looked over at the mice, and all of their eyes were on the glowing staff. Walter gulped, and as he did so, he felt himself swallowing his old self.

The cogs in his mind turned to formulate a plan.

"So," he said, "you all serve me?"

The mice squeaked yes.

"How many of you can I control? And what can you do for me?"

To an outsider, it would've been nothing but squeaking coming from the mice, but for Walter, who understood their language, he heard them say: *All of us, and anything you want, Master.*

Anything at all.

*

The next day, Walter struggled to focus on the task in front of him. He stared at the computer screen, trying to type up his report that was due next Tuesday, but all he could see in his mind's eye was mice. Mice, and rats, and hamsters, and guinea pigs.

Which gave him an idea… and made his mind wander further away from the report. Maybe last night had been some elaborate nightmare. Sure, the hole in the kitchen wall was real, no doubt about that. He had seen it this morning before leaving for work, but maybe being the mice's master had been a dream.

Walter looked at the time on his computer screen. 11:45 am. It was a little early to take his lunch break, but whatever. It's not like he was planning on doing work, and if this power was real, he'd never have to do work again. He'd quit his job.

But before he could get too excited, he had to make sure.

He rose out of his computer chair and headed for his boss's desk. His boss was a chubby guy that was perpetually red and always looked on the verge of exploding with intensity.

Walter stopped in front of his desk and said, "I'm taking my lunch break early."

His boss looked up from his computer monitor and searched his face for any signs of him being sick. "Okay?"

"I've got some stuff I want to get done before 1 o'clock," Walter said, and for no reason added, "A package I need to send out."

"Alright, but we were going to order burritos for the office today. You know—humpday and all."

In the whirlwind of the break-up and the excitement of his newfound powers, Walter had forgotten what day of the week it was. He shook his head, "That's fine, don't worry about me. I'll pick something up when I'm out."

His boss nodded and returned to work.

Walter went back to his desk, grabbed his keys off of it and then headed for the exit. The gem on the staff wasn't glowing, and that was another problem he'd have to figure out about these powers, how to activate the dang things.

*

The hamster was in its corner, chewing away at a piece of bark, minding its own business. It wasn't even aware of Walter's presence, which frustrated him. The mice seemed to have come under his control through the walls, but now here he was in front of another rodent and it paid him no attention.

He took the staff out of his shirt pocket. It was dull, turned off, "deactivated", if you will.

"Come on, work, work," he whispered to it, hoping it would do the trick.

But it didn't.

He banged the staff against the glass, and the hamster turned its head to him, but it was used to kids banging on the glass, so it turned back to gnawing on the bark.

"Work, dammit!" He said a little louder.

Nothing still.

Of course not. The incident with the mice last night had been nothing but some manic episode his mind must have created to protect him from the misery of Marcy breaking up with him.

Marcy, Marcy. He wondered if she was dating someone else by now. Probably; she was pretty. Thick brown hair, olive-colored skin, nice curvy hips, she had it all.

And he had lost it because... because why?

Because he wasn't good enough? Because he didn't say the right things? Didn't do enough to keep her satisfied? Inside and outside the bedroom?

All of the above?

In the cage, the hamster turned its head, dropping the piece of bark to the side in the process. Its black eyes peered out at the glowing gem Walter held.

It had been activated by his thoughts of Marcy. Somehow it was tied to his misery; somehow it fed off of the pain of his break-up.

That's why it had sat in his apartment for weeks without the mice in his walls going bonkers over it, because he had been happy, because the sadness hadn't awakened whatever ancient power lied inside of the gem.

Walter honed the thoughts of Marcy and all of the negative feelings that came with them into the gem, like guiding a thread through the hole of a needle.

Come... come... come, he willed the hamster.

The hamster obeyed and walked over to the glowing gem. It scratched at the glass furiously. It put its teeth against it, but couldn't get a good enough bite, so it went back to slashing at it. One of its claws splintered, and then broke against the plastic. Little droplets of blood dripped out of the wound and spilled all over the white bedding.

"Yes, yes," he said, and felt his mouth work into a smile.

No free will for the rodent. The only will it had was what he willed it to do, and right now he wanted to see how far it would go to serve him.

"Fight out of your cage, yes, yes," Walter said.

Another one of the hamster's claws broke, and more specks of blood fell onto the bedding.

"Can I help you?" A voice broke his concentration.

In one fluid motion, Walter put the key back into his pocket and spun around to see who it was. It was a girl in her late teens, wearing a pair of glasses that were stylish in an era she probably was three decades too young to know anything about.

"No, I'm just shopping around. Thank you," he said, and whirled away from her before she could say anything more.

He walked a few paces down the aisle, and then spun back around to see the girl straightening out some bags of bedding on a shelf. "That hamster in there, I think he's hurt. You might want to check on 'em."

The girl looked up at him, and her eyes grew big. For a second, he thought she somehow knew about his power, and this angered him. So he said, "That's your job, isn't it?"

The girl got up from her crouch and put her face close to the hamster's cage. She saw the bleeding claws. "You're right, he is hurt."

"Yeah," Walter said, and then continued down the aisle until he was at the end.

He turned the corner and then poked his head out from behind the shelf. Without taking his eyes off of where the girl was, he took the keys out of his pocket, staff first, and held it up in front of him. He was curious to see if there actually was no limit to what the rodents would do for him.

That bitch had interrupted what he was doing. It reminded him of when Marcy would come over when he was trying to build his sports car models and pester him with questions about things that didn't matter. *Did you ever find that polo? What do you want for breakfast tomorrow? When was the last time you cleaned your toilet bowl?*

Now that he thought about it, it should've been him who dumped her, not the other way around. She and this girl, they were a lot alike. Thin, pretty, and not much else going for them.

I bet she has a boyfriend that she bosses around. A chump that one day she'll hurt the way Marcy hurt me.

The gem glowed red, like the eyes of a rat at the end of an alley.

The girl stuck a key at the bottom of the enclosure and pulled the cabinet the cage was built into. She stuck her hand through the top and chased the hamster until it was cornered so she could pick it up.

He could feel the hamster under his control. The staff was shooting energy through his hand and down his entire body, and then shooting it at the rodent and connecting their minds as one.

He gave the hamster a command: *Bite.*

The girl screamed as the hamster sunk its teeth into the side of her hand. She threw it against the back of the cage and snatched her hand out of the cage. The hamster leapt at the spot where the girl's hand had been a second ago to bite again, but missed and kept running until it smacked against the front of the cage. The girl slammed the cabinet closed and jumped back from the enclosure.

The hamster had its teeth bared, its claws scratched at the glass. The girl looked at it with horror and puzzlement on her face. "The fuck is wrong with you?"

Walter grinned and then sent another command to the creature's tiny mind. *Relent.*

The hamster ceased baring its teeth and attacking the glass, and returned to normal. It moved away from the front of the cage and back to where its chew toy was.

The girl ran down the aisle, holding her bleeding hand, right past Walter without even noticing him and burst through the bathroom doors located at the back of the store.

So the rodents would even hurt people for him, they truly were subservient to him in every way. His experimentation was finished; he knew what he could do. Now it was time to work out the logistics of his plan.

*

They followed his every step as he paced back and forth between them. Dozens of small mice were lined up on the floor of his kitchen. They'd come together under his command as one unit to make up a bigger animal, a medium sized dog, maybe.

He held the staff in between his two fingers, it was separated from the rest of his keys. The hateful thoughts of Marcy that filled his mind made the gem glow red.

It must have been destiny, or something like it, that the powers of the staff worked in this manner.

"All of you will follow me out of the apartment. When we get to the street level, I need you to find more like you. Understand?" Walter said, then commanded them to respond.

The mice squeaked in unison, and Walter smiled in satisfaction. "Good. Now, off we go."

He led the mice out of the apartment and down the rest of the building. It was past midnight; he was sure none of the other tenants would be roaming the halls.

The rodents followed him as he went through the corridors of the apartment building and down the stairs, like a sea of fur. Like troops following their commander. Like cavalry following a king.

Like servants following a god.

*

Another night of tossing and turning, and she knew she wouldn't get enough rest to skip coffee in the morning. She'd been getting migraines from the caffeine recently and wanted to quit cold turkey, but then she dumped Walter and the bad nights of sleep had left her no choice in the mornings.

She turned and accidently kicked Frankie, who lay by her feet. He growled and then put his head back between his paws.

Her phone lit up on her bedside table, alerting her to a new text message. She looked at it, and felt a blanket of disappointment fall on top of her when she saw it was from Scott, a guy from work that she thought was just a friend up until recently. Once word got around that she wasn't seeing Walter anymore, he had been asking her out incessantly.

The text message was, of course, him asking her out tomorrow night. He had tickets to see ShowRun, but she didn't much feel like going to see a conert. Especially not with him, especially not if it would lead him on.

She put her phone on silent and then hit the rest button and lay back down. For a few seconds, she thought of calling Walter and asking him to get back with her.

No, no, Marcy. This is what you wanted.

She knew it was just temporarily loneliness because her pillowcases still smelled of his aftershave. It was faint, and she'd have to bury her face in the pillow to really get it, or move the pillow in a way that it would send the scent up her nostrils, but it was there, and it didn't help that she was feeling particularly lonely tonight.

Besides, she couldn't promise herself that down the road she wouldn't dump him again. If that were the case, she'd be playing a game of cat-and-mouse with Walter's feelings, and she didn't have it in her heart to do that.

She turned on her side and tried to go back to sleep.

*

It was rare that he was up at this hour of the night because Paul was in his mid-70s, but tonight he was determined to finish up the last hundred pages of *I, Robot*.

He stopped reading when he heard a noise outside of his apartment's door, something in the corridors—no, *somethings*—were marching toward the stairwells. A stampede.

Paul got out of his chair, feeling his old bones creak and his joints flicker with the slightest tinge of arthritic pain that the Aleve couldn't mask. He put his novel on the lamp table and went over to look through the peephole.

He saw nothing, and by now the stampeding was down the stretch of the hallway, four doors past his own. For a brief second, he considered opening the door and checking to make sure everything was alright, but decided against it and instead turned back to his recliner and his book.

Had he looked out of his door, the old man would have been surprised to see a legion of mice following Walter down the stairs of the apartment building and would have thought this was the beginning of going senile.

Perhaps it was a good thing for his health that he hadn't checked.

*

The key went into the hole, turned, and unlocked the door just as it always had. Walter grinned in a mixture of glee and relief. A part of him thought this would have been the hard part, getting into the apartment, but Marcy had fucked up by not having the locks changed after the break-up. The key to her apartment she gave to him two years ago would be her undoing now.

Not like it mattered; even if she had them changed, the rats and mice at his feet would have chewed through the damn thing at his command, but just the same, this was a good sign.

For him. Not for her.

He grinned again.

The rodents—now a mix of rats and mice, but mostly rats—followed him into the apartment. They moved in unison through the door. Not one of them was out of sync. Some walked in front of him, some walked to the side of him, and others trailed behind, protecting Walter from every which way.

He marched the rodents to the bedroom door and turned the knob slowly. He didn't want her to wake until he was in the room. He crept in, the rodents moving at the same pace he did, and stopped when he was about three feet from her bed.

"Rise and shine, sleeping beauty," Walter said.

Marcy's eyes flicked open, and she saw the shadow at the foot of her bed. She reached over her pillow and tugged the string on the lamp to turn it on. It was Walter, just as she had thought it was, but he looked different somehow.

He wasn't slouched over in a feeble attempt to hide his flabby chest and paunch; no, his posture was rigid, confident. He had a full-grown beard that made his otherwise soft face look somehow powerful.

She would have been aroused, if not for the unexpectedness of the visit. "Walt? What—what are you doing here?"

Frankie was up, his back arched and hissing. She never heard Frankie hiss in the entire time she had adopted him. This was getting stranger by the minute. Marcy sat up on the bed, and Walter moved closer, from out of the shadows and into the light of her bedside lamp.

His eyes were bloodshot red, and on his shoulder was a fat, black rat with eyes redder than his own.

"Your first mistake, Marce, was giving me this," he said, holding up the glowing staff.

"Walt?" Her eyes went to the stupid keychain he was holding up, and she hoped this was a big gag. That hope burst almost as quickly as it had come when she saw Walter's face grow even darker.

"Uh-uh, sweetie. It's too late to try to kiss and make up now," he flashed a smile at her that sent ice through her veins. "Your second mistake was not changing the locks on your door."

Frankie hissed, then swiped at something at the foot of the bed. Marcy shrank back against the wall. Hopeless and scared. Mostly scared.

"And your third, and biggest mistake, was messing with a god," Walter said.

The mice and rats jumped up on the bed. Frankie swiped at the mice coming after him, sending some of them flying back down to the floor and tearing some of them open with his claws. Their heads went flying across the bed, leaving trails of blood and tissue in their wake. But there were too many of them for the cat to fight off, and they overwhelmed him until they covered his entire body, biting and clawing at him.

Marcy watched it as a preview of what they were going to do to her. She screamed and looked away as something fell out from her cat's stomach, something long and bloody. The cat fell to its side, dead, but the mice continued to consume its flesh.

Meanwhile, rats and mice had crawled up Marcy's feet and legs. She kicked and screamed and cried, but it was futile. They were heavy on her, weighing her down and keeping her from getting out of the bed, shackling her.

The rodents swarmed on her torso and on her arms, bringing them to the side of her body. They piled on, getting heavier and heavier so that she felt like she was wearing a living, breathing straightjacket on her body.

They bit and clawed at her skin, and she knew that with each inch of flesh they tore off she was an inch closer to death.

They climbed onto her chin, and then on her face and all around her head. There were so many of them that she couldn't see anything, she couldn't even breathe. All she felt was fur and prickles of pain all over her body. There was no rhyme or reason to how it came, maybe a toe was being bit, maybe her forearm, maybe her nose.

Walter watched with fascination as his servants swarmed his ex-girlfriend. As they swarmed that bitch and ate her alive like ants eating a piece of candy on the sidewalk on a hot summer day. He couldn't believe that this power was his, and that *she* had given it to him. As inadvertent as it had been, she had granted him this power.

She had turned him into something beyond human.

When she stopped struggling underneath their attack, he called the rodents off. They jumped off of her and ran back into ranks by his feet. Some of them were sticky with blood. From their own or Marcy's or the cat's, but most remained unscathed.

On the bed, what remained of Marcy was a bloody mess of a skeleton. There were still chunks of flesh here and there, mostly on her torso, but for the most part the rodents had cleaned her bones up like a Thanksgiving turkey being cleaned for leftover sandwiches.

He didn't feel sad anymore, despite that he had loved and given everything he had to the woman this corpse used to be, he didn't feel an ounce of regret. No, in fact, he felt unsatisfied with what he did, because there was more to be done.

*

Marcy and the day he discovered his powers felt like a lifetime ago.

Every car that passed under the overpass had its headlights on because night had swallowed the last of daylight while Walter had been thinking about the last three days.

They would find Marcy's corpse any day now, and he'd be suspect number one, which meant he'd be fleeing out of the state soon.

That was fine by him, because there were others who deserved to see their end, even more than Marcy. There were others in his life who had wronged him, and now he had the power to pay them back for the torment.

Turning away from the bridge, he headed home. A legion of rodents followed close behind him. Ready to serve and die for their god.

PILLS

"It's not just my shoulder anymore, Hank," Barry said as he watched the Sprite and vodka fizzle to the top of the glass while the ice cubes tinkled against each other. "It's like my damn soul is being sucked right out of me."

Hank put the hose back on its hook and the bottle back on the shelf. He grabbed a rag from a bucket sitting on the corner of the counter and started cleaning last night's crumbs of breaded wings and hamburgers. "I already told you, two Aleves a day, and then again at night."

"I tried that. I've tried doubling that, tripling that. Shit, I'd do four times the recommended dosage if I wasn't scared of ODing on the junk." Barry picked his drink up and took a sip. It was stronger than the last one. *Maybe bitching and complaining does get you somewhere.* Barry thought.

"You go to the doctor's?" Hank asked.

"Yeah, I did," Barry said.

"And?"

"And get a load of this, he prescribed me Xanax."

"Xanax? The anxiety medicine?"

"That's right. Anxiety medicine for shoulder pain."

"Sounds like bullshit, to me. Why not give you pain pills?" Hank asked.

Barry shook his head. "He said they can't find anything wrong with me. X-rays came back negative. They sent me to a physical therapist and even he couldn't find anything wrong."

Hank stopped cleaning and leaned back with a hand on his hip to get a good look at Barry. The kid he met when he was twenty-one was almost forty now, had gone through two marriages, had no kids, and lived in a one-bedroom apartment by himself, not even a beagle or a pet hamster, and he had no girlfriend that Hank knew of. Perhaps the doctor was on to something in thinking that it was his own mind making up pain to mask his less-than-desirable circumstances, to distract him from it.

"Did the Xanax do anything?" Hank asked.

"No, all it did was make me lie on the couch all day and listen to my upstairs neighbor pacing back and forth between chapters."

"Between chapters? He's a writer?"

"Yeah," Barry said. Usually his neighbor's insomniac pacing back and forth bugged him, but after popping the Xanax pills, the sound of the floorboards squeaking had been as calming as a late-night jazz tune.

"Sounds like your apartment building is filled with a bunch of weirdos," Hank said, and went back to cleaning the counter.

Barry smiled, but he couldn't help to feel a little hurt by the comment, considering this wasn't his fault. And also, Hank ran a bar that was known as the alcoholics' clubhouse by everyone on the west side of the city, so he didn't have much room to judge.

"I'm looking at a pay cut at work soon, too, if this doesn't get any better," Barry said, taking another sip of his drink.

"Because you won't be able to take out the dogs?" Hank asked.

"Yeah," Barry stretched his right arm out as if he was pitching a softball, "it's on my good arm, and the German Shepherds kill me."

"Those bad boys must have some pull to them."

"Hellacious," Barry said, staring down at his drink, "everything seems to be hellacious ever since this pain started up."

The door to the bar swung open, and in came two men sporting raggedy coats. They shook off snow from their old boots and proceeded to hang their winter garb on the coat hook at the front of the establishment.

"I'm sorry to hear that," Hank replied, and he was sorry, but his focus had turned to his regulars.

They still wore the same clothes they did back when Barry used to hang out at the Wolf Eye Tavern regularly. The only difference was their shitty clothes were shittier: the holes in them bigger and the stains darker.

"What happened to the other two? They die of alcohol poisoning?" Barry pointed his thumb over his shoulder to the two members of the Goonsquad— a name that Barry and Hank used as a joke to describe the four alcoholics that visited the Wolf Eye daily.

Hank shook his head. "Nope. Fred is in jail, and Tom checked himself into rehab two weeks ago."

Barry picked up his glass, suddenly not wanting it, but took a big gulp of it anyway. "I see nothing has changed around the Wolf Eye."

Hank shrugged and went over to the fridge where the 40s of the Goonsquad's favorite malt liquor were always kept cool for them. Opening the door, he said to Barry, "As long as they keep the cash comin' in steady and don't smell like cat piss, I'm fine with it."

Before Barry could respond to this, he felt an arm squeeze around his shoulder. As gentle as the squeeze was, it didn't stop the pain from shooting through him like a jolt of lightning.

He wanted to yelp, but he tapped all of his willpower to keep from doing so and blinked away the tears that were building up, hoping neither of the two men had seen them.

"Say, if it ain't our old pal, Barry," the man embracing him said.

Barry knew who it was from the greeting—but mostly the stench. "Hey, Mitch, nice to see you again."

Mitch grinned, showing a gold tooth in a mouth full of missing teeth. He was the unofficial leader of the Goonsquad.

The other man, Dave, walked over to the other side of Barry and leaned against the counter, ignoring the stool for the moment.

Hank came over, dropped off the two Colt 45s that would get them started, and then went into the back room.

Thanks Hank, leaving me here with these knuckleheads. Barry thought, but then an idea started to bloom in his mind.

"What you drinking there?" Mitch looked at his Sprite and vodka mix and laughed. It was a drink-induced laugh. "Are there bubbles in it? Man, you a yuppie now or something?"

Dave had sat down on the stool the moment Hank had dropped the bottles off and had already drunk a quarter of his malt liquor. "You a doctor?"

Barry smiled at them. For some reason, they thought getting a college degree meant going from rags to riches after the graduation ceremony. If only that were true; Barry wouldn't be here trying to drink his pain away.

"Why haven't you stopped by sooner? You forgot about us poor folk?" Mitch continued.

"No, it's not that Mitch, it's just that I've been busy with work and all," Barry said.

Mitch clapped him on the shoulder, and then went to town on his malt liquor.

In the corner of the bar, an oscillating fan rattled. It was on despite the winter weather because the heating system in the Wolf Eye was either off or on full blast, and right now it was off, turning the place into a sweatbox. In the back room, Hank was opening and shuffling around boxes.

The three men sat in silence for a few minutes, until Barry leaned in toward Mitch and in a low voice said, "Say, Mitch, you still got them percs?"

Mitch seemed taken aback by this, but a sly grin formed on his face. "Oh, you're coming to the dark side, huh?"

"Not quite. I've got a pain in my shoulder that's killing me," Barry said.

"Ain't you rich?" Dave said, overhearing despite the whisper. "Can't you afford to go to the doctor's?"

Barry addressed his question but kept his focus on Mitch. "The doctor can't find anything wrong with me and won't prescribe me pain meds. I've been taking Aleve, but you know that's nothing compared to the good stuff."

"Damn right it isn't," Mitch said, reaching into the pocket of his sweatshirt. "I got 'em if you have cash."

Barry took out his wallet and held out a ten-dollar bill he intended to use for Indian tonight, but was willing to sacrifice. "How much does this get me?"

"More importantly, how much does that get *me*," Mitch said, and let out another drunk laugh. The Goonsquad didn't do hard drugs like percs, but they weren't above selling them to get cash for more booze. "I'll give you five pills for that."

Barry folded the bill and set it on the counter. "Done deal."

Hank was back behind the counter and stocking the fridge behind the bar with PBR for the college kids that would come in later that night. He eyed the ten-dollar bill suspiciously and then met Barry's eyes. *I get it, kid, you're desperate.*

Barry nodded to him, and Hank nodded back before returning to his work.

Mitch grabbed the ten dollars and put the bottle of pills in Barry's hand.

"You think you can get me more, if I need it?" Barry asked. He got up to leave, no longer comfortable with the whole deal.

It may have been the alcohol's effects on him, but suddenly the whirring of the fan was grating his ears and drinking with the Goonsquad was making him feel pathetic.

"Whoa, pal, you heading out already?" Mitch asked, sounding hurt.

Dave leaned in toward them and with a stupid grin on his face said, "he must have a dissertation to work on."

They both laughed, and Barry tried to hide his surprise that a self-appointed Bigfoot hunter like Dave—evidenced by the trucker hat he wore with an embroidered Bigfoot—not only had that word in his rolodex, but knew how to use it correctly.

"Something like that," Barry said when their laughter died down.

He headed for the coat hooks and bundled up. Turning back toward the counter, he meant to wave to Hank, but he had gone into the back to prep the grill for lunch hour, so instead he waved to the Goonsquad, whose response was another roar of laughter. The malt liquor must have been working already.

Barry pushed the door open, grateful for the cold even though it sliced at his earlobes like an invisible razor.

*

The percs didn't work, but Barry had stopped by the liquor store on his way home from the Wolf Eye Tavern to finish what the Goonsquad had interrupted. He got blackout drunk, not remembering or caring if percs and alcohol weren't meant to be mixed.

*

His phone buzzing on his nightstand woke him up. Peering through the slits of the blinds, he could see that the sky outside was still purple. That was one of the parts he hated most about winter, waking up before the sun did.

He rolled over on his stomach and saw it was 8:10 am.

Who the hell is texting me at this hour?

But as soon as he touched his phone he remembered what day it was—it was hard to keep track of the days when off from work for the last two weeks—Wednesday, the only day of the week that he and Carrie could meet in the mornings for breakfast.

Barry lay in bed for a moment, feeling as stiff as an air-dried towel and holding his phone inches away from his face, trying to come up with an excuse that sounded better than: *hey, I got fucking plastered last night and can barely get out of bed. Sorry sweetie.*

Then he read her text messages:

7:45am
Good morning, Ginger Ale, can't wait to see you today. ;)

8:04am
You're not canceling on me, are you Goose?

Those were the two nicknames she had for him; Ginger Ale because of his hair and Goose because of his profession.

The cute text messages made him forget about the shoulder pain, the ghost of a stomachache from the whiskey, and the *knock-knock* in the back of his head from the mini-hangover so much so that he sprang out of bed.

... And was reminded of the pain as his shoulder moved in a way it shouldn't have. Since Mitch and company weren't around to judge him, he let out a howl of agony.

"Ow, fuck, that hurts!"

He fell back into bed, curled into fetal position and bit his pillow. Tears welled up in his eyes as the pain in his shoulder worsened by the second.

It felt like an eternity when it began to subside, but in reality, the big hand on his alarm clock had only moved one tick by the time he was ready to try getting out of bed again. More careful than the first time, Barry got out of bed and looked for his phone. He picked it up off the floor and sent Carrie a text:

8:11am
I'm going to be fashionably late. I hope you don't mind, see you in a bit.

As quickly as his pained body would allow him, Barry threw on a pair of jeans that was on the verge of needing to be washed, put on his snow boots, and then a wool sweater hanging on the rim of his hamper that Carrie had given him for Christmas two weeks ago.

Dressed, he headed out of his apartment.

*

The frozen crust of the snow crunched underneath his feet as he walked through areas on the sidewalk that hadn't yet been cleaned. As per usual, the snowfall had been exaggerated by the news, and there had only been an inch of snow, so it wasn't too bad navigating from his apartment to the café.

Of course, I could slip and fall and mess my shoulder up with my luck. Barry thought.

Once he was underneath the awning of Bella's Café, he assumed himself safe. He pulled the door open and the accompanying jingle reassured him he had made it in one piece.

Barry shook the snow off his boots onto the rug and let the coziness of the place settle around him. It wasn't just the warmth from the heater, it was the smell of the freshly baked bread and pouring coffee that warmed him.

"Hey, welcome to Bella's, how many?" A young girl he had never seen before said from behind the hostess podium. She had on a smile and thick-rimmed glasses. Both looked too unnatural for her face.

Barry scanned the dining area over her shoulder and spotted Carrie sitting at a booth, sipping on a latte and watching the morning news on one of the café's TVs. Her back was to him, but her fire-red hair was unmistakable.

He shook his head, "I'm here to meet someone, thank you though."

The hostess's smile grew bigger and faker as she put the menu back on a shelf and then slipped out from behind the podium.

Barry smiled at her and then walked down to the fourth booth.

"I thought I was getting stood up," Carrie said when she saw him, a grin on her face.

He hung his coat and hat on the hooks on the side of the booth and got into the seat across from her. He let out a sigh, but what he really wanted was to yell.

"What's wrong?" Carrie asked, the grin disappearing from her face.

Barry sighed again. "Do I look like shit or something? The hostess asked how many were in my party and grabbed only *one* menu."

Carrie bit her lip, but a slight giggle escaped between them. "You do look a little worn, Goose."

She put her mug down and reached over the table to give his cheek a squeeze. Her fingers were warm and smelled of the gingerbread lotion he had given her for Christmas. He smiled.

"Seriously, though," Barry said, "I know you're probably tired of hearing me complain about this, but this damn shoulder is still killing me."

"Guess I'll have to give you a nice shoulder rub this weekend, huh?" She said, picking up her mug and blowing into it.

Her arms moved up to guide the mug to her lips, giving Barry a peek at the cleavage her green dress sported. Carrie was wholesome and rarely wore outfits that were revealing or low cut, and that's what made it doubly exciting when she did.

"Nice dress," Barry said, unable to help himself.

He saw her smile over the top of the mug, and she still was smiling when she set it down. "I went thrifting yesterday, you really like it?"

Barry nodded. And before the conversation could continue, the waitress came over to take their orders. Carrie ordered her usual fruit oatmeal, and Barry ordered a stack of pancakes. He felt like he had been putting on some pounds since he took off from work due to his shoulder, so he opted out of the free whipped cream.

The waitress left, and Carrie broke the seconds of silence it took for her to be out of earshot's distance. "How long's it been now?"

"My shoulder?" Barry asked.

"Yeah," she said.

Barry did the math in his head (which he was never good at, that's why he had gone to school for English) and said, "I guess like three months."

"My God, Barry, and it doesn't feel any better? Like, at all?"

"Nope. Hurts worse, if anything," Barry admitted.

"You said your doctor prescribed you Xanax, right? Did that help at all?"

Barry shook his head. "Should I go see another doctor?"

Carrie shrugged. "It wouldn't hurt to try. I mean, Xanax for shoulder pain... what the heck is that about?"

"Yeah, I said the same thing when he suggested it." Barry drummed his fingers on his knee, and Carrie caught the movement even though his arm was under the table.

"Uh oh, come on, spit it out, Ginger Ale," Carrie said.

Barry stopped drumming and looked at her, feeling like a kid caught with his hand in the cookie jar. After two years of knowing him, she knew his every tick and what they meant. "There's one more thing."

And it was odd that he was embarrassed to tell her this, considering she knew of his insurance policy on his *Batman* action figure collection. Barry rubbed the back of his neck. "I'm so desperate I even tried acupuncture."

Carrie put her hand over her mouth as she laughed, and a small snort came out in the midst of the fit of laughter. Barry felt his face turn as red as his hair—or her hair, for that matter.

When the laughing stopped, Carrie reached over and grabbed his hand. "I'm sorry, I didn't mean to laugh that hard—this coffee sure is strong. But, I'm assuming that didn't work?"

"Nope, just got prickled with pins for no reason," Barry said, his shoulders slumping.

The waitress returned with their food. They came here often enough, about once every two or three weeks, and every time Barry was surprised at how fast his pancakes were brought out. Microwaves were a godsend.

The waitress asked if they needed anything else, they both said no, and she went away, leaving them to their breakfast.

Carrie was thin because she ran ten miles every morning, and her appetite was as active as her lifestyle. She held the bowl inches away from her face so that the spoon wouldn't have to travel far to reach her mouth. As she scarfed down her oatmeal, Barry couldn't help but compare her to the stray cat outside of his apartment he sometimes fed. They both ate with the same vigorous desperation.

"Hungry, much?" he asked, cutting the first bite of his pancake.

"I ran fifteen miles this morning, don't judge me," she said, not slowing down even a notch to talk.

"Fifteen?" Barry said.

She set the bowl down and grabbed a napkin to wipe at the sides of her mouth. "Oh yeah, I forgot to tell you, I'm working a double tonight."

Barry was taken back, considering she worked nights, so a double shift meant she'd have to be in to work at—

"I gotta be in at the office at 10." Carrie finished the thought for him.

Barry looked up at the TV across their table, where a news anchor with a head of gray hairs and an economist with a comical bowtie discussed the ins-and-outs of small business. At the bottom of the screen, the ticker displayed the time: 9:40 am.

"You only have twenty minutes to get to work, though," Barry said. "Or am I that bad at math?"

"I know, I already called the office and told them I would be a little late, but I'm leaving as soon as I finish this bowl." She picked up her latte and took a sip. "You can have whatever is left of this."

"No thanks," Barry replied.

Carrie peered down at her wrist where a thin watch told her the time. "Oh shoot, it's later than I thought."

"Yeah," Barry said.

She finished off her oatmeal and slammed down the bowl like she was a food eating champion, and then opened her purse and started rifling through it, looking for her wallet.

"No," Barry said, "I got it. Go ahead and go to work."

Carrie stopped mid-dig and smiled at him. "You sure?"

It was going to hurt his pocket, but he never let up a chance to make her happy. "Yeah, I'm sure."

"Great," she stuffed her oversized wallet back into her oversized purse and then pinched his cheek before getting out of the booth. "I gotta run. Literally."

She waved her foot in front of him to draw his attention, and Barry saw she was wearing the brightest blue running shoes he had ever seen. The combination of that and the pretty green dress made him burst out in laughter. "What the heck? Did you get dressed in the dark?"

Carrie fake-frowned at him, and her shoulders slumped. "You don't like? They were on discount and the prettiest blue I've ever seen."

"They look fine enough, but they don't quite match the dress," Barry said, and looked at the dress and shoes once more to see if he had missed something that brought them together. A buckle or laces, perhaps. Nope, still discombobulated on a second glance.

"I have a change of pair in the office," Carrie said. "I have another fifteen miles to run from here to work."

"You didn't drive here?" Barry nearly jumped out of the booth.

She shook her head, her hair flying back and forth on her head. "Nope, I'll be pooped by the time I finish my shift, which means I better get in all the exercise before work."

"God," Barry said. "Well, you better go then."

"Mhm," Carrie bent down and pecked his cheek. "See you this weekend, Goose. And make sure you don't put your underwear on inside-out."

Barry chuckled. "Thanks, I'll try to remember. See ya."

Carrie waved, and then turned to leave the café. He watched her go through the door, and before the bell finished its jingle, she was running down the sidewalk.

She wasn't exactly his girlfriend—in fact he wasn't sure just *what* they were, because her bipolar disorder didn't let her commit to a relationship, but he thought when they finally decided to make it official he'd ask her to move out of her parents' house and move in with him.

Between him with his odd shoulder pain, his insomniac neighbor who paced back and forth all day and night, and her manic episodes of unrelenting exercise, Hank's comment that his apartment building was full of weirdos would ring more true when that day came.

If it comes, Barry thought, sliding the mug of coffee in front of him. He sighed, and looked down at his reflection in the liquid.

Things hadn't been going so bad until this shoulder pain started up and he had to take a cut in hours. Rent was around the corner, and he'd be lucky to have money to go out with Carrie this weekend. Maybe he'd have to call up his cokehead dad and beg him for money, after all.

"Screw that, I'd rather shoot myself," Barry muttered.

He thought he had said it to himself, but then a voice from behind him responded, "I don't think that will be necessary."

Barry thought it was the waitress, but when he turned, he saw an old man in the last booth of the café sitting by himself. The old man had dusty gray hair pressed underneath a hat with a brim so small it failed to do the one job a brim was supposed to do.

He waved to him. The hand was bigger than Barry would have thought the scrawny old man would possess, and the fingers were long, giving the illusion of a white spider waving its legs at him. The old man's face twisted into a grin.

"I couldn't help but overhear your conversation with the pretty lady," the old man admitted.

Barry coughed and looked around. At some point between when he had sat down with Carrie and when this old man called to him, the café had emptied out. He remembered at least two other tables had been occupied, and now their booths were the only ones being used.

He looked to the front of the café, where the waitresses were huddled together in a gossip circle, while the hostess who hadn't yet passed her initiation tests into the club of chatty Cathys pretended not to listen and instead cleaned a table nearby.

Barry turned back to the old man and said, "That's okay."

The old man waved his hand at him, this time in a *come, join me* gesture. "I think I can solve your problem."

He wasn't sure if he wanted to run out of the place, scream for help, or if he was intrigued by this proposition, but he felt his butt rise up underneath him. "What?"

"Your shoulder hurts, right?"

Barry got out of the booth and was walking over to join the old man before he realized what was happening. He slid into the booth and glanced around, making sure that no one was within hearing distance. Even though no one was, he leaned closer to the old man and said, "Yeah, what do you know about this? You had the same problem before?"

The old man shook his head, "Despite my age, my body is very able. I do, however, help out people that are in your predicament."

"What are you? Some sort of witch doctor?" Barry asked.

The old man laughed. "If it makes you feel better to call me that, sure."

Before Barry could respond, the old man reached into his duster jacket and pulled something out, but he held it hidden in his broad hand. "What's your name, boy? I heard the girl call you Goose?"

"Barry. Goose is a nickname."

The old man nodded. "A fine name. Anyway, in my hand I hold a cure for your troubles—sort of. You'll have to do something by the week's end to really be freed of your pain."

This was getting weirder by the minute, but Barry was so desperate that he'd be willing to buy from one of those infomercials if they promised to fix his shoulder for three easy payments of $39.99.

"Okay, show me what you got, Doc," Barry said, fidgeting.

The old man flashed a grin, and for a split second, Barry thought he saw a fang. It was actually a tooth that was sharp as a dagger, not quite a fang, but the effect was still there and the hairs on his arm rose.

The old man uncurled his fingers and on his palm was a small bottle full of pills. They were all different colors, like Flintstones vitamins.

"Please tell me that's not Xanax," Barry said.

"Xanax? No, and if I were you I'd never go back to that kook who prescribed you anxiety medicine for pain."

Barry shrugged. "I figured he learned a thing or two at med school about this stuff."

"Your problem is something they don't teach at med school, I assure you of that." The old man winked.

"Okay, then, what are these pills?"

"Let's call them magic in a bottle, why don't we?"

"Now I'm intrigued. How much for them?"

"How much? You mean money?"

"Yes, I'm sure you're not just some altruistic holistic doctor who does this for his karma—unless you are, in which case, I'm sure these are just sugar pills and will respectfully decline."

The old man's face broadened into another smile. "I'm not looking for money. I'm asking for something a little pricier than that."

Barry chortled. "Like what? My soul?"

The old man's eyes flashed, and he leaned back in the booth. "A life full of pain or a way to cure it, the choice is yours, Barry."

The old man put the bottle in the middle of the table. Barry noticed for the first time that there wasn't anything on the table except for the napkin holder, a bottle of Sriracha, and another bottle of hot sauce.

There was no suggestion of the old man having ordered anything to eat or drink. Not even a ring where a glass of water may have once sat. Only the bottle of pills.

The old man started to get out of the booth, and Barry said, "Wait, you didn't name your price."

Standing next to him, the old man said, "Take it or leave it, Barry. The price is insignificant compared to the pain you feel, and it'll only get worse. Take it from an expert."

With that, the old man's shadow moved away from Barry, and he heard his boots stamping across the hardwood floor, leaving him alone.

"An expert," Barry repeated, "expert? Expert at what?"

He grabbed the bottle, the pills inside rattled. He rolled it in his hand and saw that there was a sticker with handwriting on the back of it. It read:

Take ONE. And ONLY ONE a day.

Barry unscrewed the lid and peered into the pile of pills. It was like looking inside a packet of Skittles. He put the bottle into his jeans pocket and was about to get up when another voice surprised him.

"Sun getting into your eyes?" This time it was the waitress, and she was leaning over the booth he had been sitting at with Carrie, twirling the bar that closed the blinds shut.

Barry took another glance about the place, feeling like a man who had just come out of a meth lab with a stash of goodies, and smiled at her. "No, just catching up with an old teacher of mine."

"Oh, okay." The waitress wasn't able to hide the slight rise in her eyebrow before turning away and heading back to the kitchen.

Barry felt his face grow hot, and he wanted nothing more than to get out of here. He fished his wallet out of his jeans and took out two twenties. Walking back to his original booth, he put them on the table, threw his coat on, and darted for the door.

The hostess told him to have a good day, and he waved to her as he pushed through the front door. Above him the door jingled, and for a second, his mind turned to the thought that he never heard the bell when the old man had left the place.

*

Six days later, and the pain in his shoulder remained. He hadn't told Carrie about the encounter with the mysterious old man, because... well, quite frankly, he was worried she'd make fun of him. And to further keep this secret buried, he had transferred the colorful pills into an empty Folger's can, which he now held in his hands as he stared at himself in the bathroom mirror.

He hadn't been eating. The pain in his shoulder somehow had taken away his appetite. Carrie had made him French toast Sunday morning, and he had lodged it down his throat so as to not disappoint her, but that had been the biggest meal he'd eaten since.

His pale skin looked like it had a tinge of yellow—or maybe it was that there was more light in the bathroom since Carrie had replaced the blown-out bulbs after a month of him forgetting to do it. His cheekbones were more pronounced than before; of that he was sure. Barry ran his hands over his stomach and felt less dough and more ribs than he was used to, but it wasn't a good thing, because he also felt weak.

He looked down at the last pill in the tin can. "They haven't done shit."

Not even made him dizzy or throw up to at least give him some hope that he hadn't been tricked into taking sugar pills out of desperation. But so far, that seemed to be the case.

"Oh well," Barry plucked out the last pill and stuck it in his mouth. He rolled it around in his tongue to get it wet before he turned the faucet on and cupped some water into his mouth.

He swallowed the last pill, feeling somehow dumber that he took all seven of them, and shut the bathroom light off. He headed back into his bedroom, and went to sleep.

*

He awoke to birds on a powerline chirping outside of his window. His phone lit up from an incoming text message on his nightstand. He rolled out of bed, noting that his shoulder felt... heavy, and grabbed his phone.

Reading the text message, he realized this was the second time in a row he had forgotten about meeting up with Carrie at the café. The text message read:

Duck, duck, Goose. Hope you didn't forget about me AGAIN.

"Oh shit," Barry looked at the time, 8:45 am, which meant Carrie had already been at the café (if she hadn't already left) for forty-five minutes.

Barry threw on a pair of sweatpants lying by his bed and ran into the bathroom to brush his teeth. When he got in front of the mirror, he stopped. He thought it was a shadow at first glance, but that thought was quickly replaced by the thought that his shoulder blade had swelled up. Even from the front, Barry could see the purple mound sticking out from his back.

"What in the hell?" Barry turned to the side to get a better look at what it was.

When he saw it, he nearly screamed his head off, but the scream never came because he was astonished into silence. The mound on his back was not a shadow or his shoulder swelling up, at all; it was the top of a head.

Out from his right shoulder, an infant-sized being clung to his body, attached to him from a straw-like organ protruding from its mouth, connecting it and his own body as one.

What did that old man do to me?

He could feel his heart drumming in his ears, and with each beat, he saw the straw in the being's mouth pump like a vein. The thing was feeding off of him, sucking his soul out of him. Barry glanced at himself in the mirror for a second and saw that his skin did indeed have a yellow tinge to it. It was no trick of the light.

And this damn thing the old man had attached to him was doing it.

Then, the words of the old man echoed through his head... *I hold a cure for your troubles—sort of. You'll have to do something by the week's end to really be freed of your pain.*

No, the pain that—not coincidentally, was concentrated where the being was attached to him, had been haunting him long before he met the old man at Bella's.

Those pills, the *magic in a bottle* as the old man had called them, had only made him be able to see it.

The old man had seen the being attached on his shoulder... somehow.

He turned to the side again, despite that his stomach would twist into knots at the sight of this bloodsucking entity, and looked at the pulsing straw.

Right there, that's how he'd get rid of it.

He went into the kitchen and grabbed the sharpest knife he found in the drawer, and then returned to the bathroom. Breathing in deeply, he once again turned to get a good look at where exactly the organ was attached.

He held the blade over the middle of the straw, and cut. The flesh and tissue of the organ made popping sounds as the knife ripped through it. Black blood began to spurt out from the gash like a fluid line in a car had been cut.

The organ wasn't thick, but there was a lot of blood. It sprayed all over the wall, on the vanity, in the sink, on the mirror.

Barry cut, and cut, and cut until he felt the final pop of the straw breaking off.

The being's head lolled backward, and its mouth opened and eyes closed tight. Barry had been preparing himself for a howling scream the entire time he had been cutting, but no sound ever came out.

Once this was done, Barry noticed that the creature was also attached to him by its hands and feet, so he reached back and grabbed it by the waist. Its body felt like a bag of gummy bears that had sat out in the backseat of the car for too long on a summer day, and with disgust, Barry pried the creature off of him.

It kicked and punched the air like a newborn, blood splashed everywhere. Barry held the knife over its chest, ready to stab it in the heart, but he couldn't find an opening between its swipes.

The creature continued clawing at the air and Barry continued watching, until it ran out of energy. Removed from its source of life, it died.

Barry threw the carcass into the trashcan and tied the bag closed. As he did this, he noted that the pain in his shoulder was gone. He went into the kitchen and dumped the bag into the bigger trashcan.

Standing in the middle of his kitchen he rotated his right arm in a circle, bracing himself for the shock of pain—but just like the being's harrowing screams, the pain never came. He smiled and thanked the mysterious old man.

Now he didn't have to worry about his shoulder anymore. He'd go to work tomorrow and tell his boss that he was back in business, to give him the dog to take out, hell, give him *two* dogs to take out.

He was back.

The only worry he had now was explaining to Carrie why he was late.

And making sure his underwear wasn't on inside-out.

...And the worry that he had just made a deal with the devil. But for that one, he'd have a (painless) life's length to sort out.

I AM THE END-BRINGER

[Selected pages from the journal of Jeremy Strickland]

August 22nd, 2016

I'm sick of being called fat by everyone. Even people at my school who say they're my friends call me fat, but I'm especially sick of being called fat by the jocks. Don, who's fatter than me, calls me fat, and they all laugh when he does it.

Each time they do, it cuts deep. I hate being this way, but I can't find the right motivation to lose weight because it's easier to not lose it. I've tried doing it in the past many times, and I feel pathetic every time I exercise. I can barely jump rope for twenty seconds without having to suck wind. I can barely run for more than a minute before I feel like toppling over on the ground like an overworked donkey.

I hate it, and I hate myself for not being good enough to do it.

I was reading on some bodybuilding website today of other fat kids like me who've had success in their attempts. I have to admit, every bone in my body was jealous as I read, but another part of me started to feel motivated. They all had the usual spiel: drink lots of water, eat healthier, exercise more, blah blah blah.

Yeah, that's all good and well, but I tried doing that before and it was just too hard so I gave up on it. One thing that someone posted on the thread was that they kept a journal and tracked their pounds and that doing that made it feel like keeping track of your RPG character, but instead of a mage that you're working on, you're working on (and I quote) "yourself to look and feel sexy as fuck."

The guy sounds like he turned into a real shithead, but I'm going to take his advice because he honestly looked worse than me in his before pictures. So, here it is, my log journal of me trying to lose weight. I guess one part that will keep me going for as long as possible is the dread of not wanting the last entry to be "I quit. I failed yet again. Back to my Ho Hos I go."

Let's see.

August 29th, 2016

Well, a week later and I'm still waking up sore. It's everywhere, not just my calves and thighs. My back is feeling it, too. I guess I'm pushing myself the way they say you're supposed to because I run for fifteen minutes or until I feel like I'm about to explode, whichever comes first. Embarrassingly, it's usually the latter at about the eleven-minute mark.

I feel pathetic. The other day I overheard these girls at the grocery store (I was picking up soy milk to make myself 'healthy' chocolate milk—don't judge me, Journal) talking about their runtimes. They were prepping for a 5k.

And here I am, dreading the first twenty minutes of my day tomorrow writing this stupid journal. Oh well, hopefully one day I'll be in the position of those girls, and I'll inspire someone like me to keep pushing, because that's what I plan on doing. I don't think I'll be giving up this time. I've lost almost 10 lbs. already!

Alright, time to grab a snack and hit the sheets before the twenty minutes of hell tomorrow.

Good night.

September 12ᵗʰ, 2016

I'm still at it, and 20 lbs. down. I see myself in the mirror, and I start to think that maybe a few good-looking features were hidden underneath all of my blubber.

I think in some way I'm turning into that douchebag on that bodybuilding website I wrote about before.

God, I hope not.

November 4ᵗʰ, 2016

This is the longest I've ever kept this up, and since this is my personal journal and no one will ever read it (I hope), I'll write the number on the scale that inspired me to go through with this this long.

255.

Yup, I was even too embarrassed to write that down in the confines of my own home, but here I am sitting under 220 lbs.! I'm at 219, and I couldn't be more proud of myself. Heck, I'm starting to feel so confident in myself that today at the library I approached a girl that I thought was cute. Turns out she works at the pizza shop down the street from my house.

I don't really like their food, but I do like Madeline. So maybe I'll pay them a visit on my cheat day and get some mozzarella sticks, or buffalo strips, or fries drizzled with ranch... or, dang, I'm hungry.

November 22nd, 2016

I'm down to 207 lbs., sweet.

I went out with Madeline tonight. We went to an indoor mini-golf course and then to a pastry shop near her house. We got hot chocolate and shared a giant éclair, after that we walked around her neighborhood and talked while our teeth chattered.

Then we sat around on her porch until my mom came to pick me up. We kissed.

My first date and my first kiss all in the same night. I'd say this losing weight thing is turning out great.

December 1st, 2016

Well, tomorrow I'm off from school for a week. Me and my mom are going out of town to visit my aunt Cathy who lives in the countryside. It's usually boring because all of the kids around are too young for me to play with. My little cousin is the youngest. I think he still wears diapers.

Oh well, at least it'll give me a chance to exercise more. Plus, my aunt Cathy is really nice and bakes a great apple pie. Mmm, apple pie.

Time to go pack my stuff.

December 2nd, 2016

It's almost midnight and I didn't exercise today. On top of that I ate four slices of my aunt's pie and sat around playing video games all day, so yeah, I'm feeling pretty chunky right now.

On a better note, my aunt's boyfriend, Joe, got a raise at work last month and he and Aunt Cathy decided to surprise us with gifts when we got to their house.

He bought an Xbox for the den in the basement that he said I could play any time I'm over. For my mom they got some earrings in the shape of ducks. Yeah, kind of weird, but my mom has this thing about ducks. You should see our house. Our bathroom wallpaper is covered in ducks, duck salt and pepper shakers, ducks on the welcome mats, it's kind of ridiculous.

In private my mom said that Aunt Cathy knows how to pick them, because the earrings they gave her are real gold. She winked when she said it. I'm guessing this was some odd, roundabout way of saying that Joe's a good guy.

Cool.

But yeah, this place might not be so good for my losing weight venture. I'll try to turn it around, but… video games and apple pie might damper my streak.

December 8th, 2016

Okay, it's the 6th straight day that I didn't exercise. I just went back to the logs and realized I'm making every excuse in the book to sit cooped up inside and play video games instead of exercising. I did pack a bunch of running gear (that's still neatly and tidily packed away at the bottom of my suitcase), but tomorrow is our last day here, and I'm planning on going out on a high note.

We drove down into "town" as the locals call it for some Christmas light festival they hold around this time every year. On our way there, I saw a pretty nice road that looked like it might be fun to run. It's windy and has some small hills, so tomorrow first thing in the morning I'm going for a run.

Can't go back to being a fat kid, no way.

December 9th, 2016

I'm sitting here in my Aunt Cathy's guest bedroom, at the desk in the corner of the room. There's an alarm clock with big green numbers on it, and they read 11:50 pm, so it's almost the 10th. I didn't go for the run early in the morning. I turned on the Xbox and told myself I'd only play for an hour and then go run, but then an hour turned into two hours, then three turned into four, and four turned into the rest of the day.

I feel guilty right now.

Everyone is asleep; I can hear my mom lightly snoring in the room next to me. It's dark out, but I'm tired of making excuses. It's what I've been doing my entire life, so I'm going to go run as soon as I finish writing this entry.

Actually, as soon as I finish writing this sentence.

December 10th, 2016

It's 3 am. I came back from the run over an hour ago. I wish I would have never gone on it. Something happened that [*scratched out illegible writing has been omitted from transcript*]

I thought I'd feel better if I wrote it down, but I can't bring myself to. I think I might take a break from logging my days.

December 15th, 2016

I'm back journal, did you miss me? Probably not. I'm going to write about what happened that night eventually, but first I want to write about this dream I had last night.

I was lying down on a table that was cold. The whole room was cold. Cold and bright, to the point where I could feel the muscles around my eyes straining to squint against the brightness even in real life. There were two figures hovering above me. At first their features were hidden behind shadows cast from the other objects in the room, but then one got closer.

He wore a surgical mask over the bottom half of his gray face. I could see veins and wrinkles running along its skin like the grooves of a raisin. The two almond-shaped eyes that peered into mine took up most of the surface of the face.

The other head came closer to me, and it looked exactly the same. Maybe more wrinkles and more veins, but other than that pretty much the same. This figure held a pair of scissors, and there was blood dripping off of them.

My blood.

I looked down at my body, and saw I was lying naked. There was a giant paper towel over my body, and where my stomach was there was a big blotch of red.

I tried to scream, but my mouth had been sewn shut. I tried to jump out of the table and run away, but my body wouldn't budge. In my sleep, in real life, I could feel myself kicking and screaming, but the dream version of me was unresponsive to my will.

The two heads returned behind the shadows, and then I woke up. I was drenched in sweat, and even worse drenched in thoughts that there was something more to the dream.

I went down to the kitchen and grabbed a cold glass of water, and then when I came back I finally took out the journal to write this all down. And here I am. I'm going to try to sleep again.

December 16th, 2016

The same dream again. Only this time instead of scissors it was a scalpel. And this time when I looked down at my body, I saw something poking out from the middle of the paper towel. No, poking out from my body. It was about the size of an adult's middle finger and bulbous at the top.

I woke up screaming. I don't know what the hell is going on with me, but I think it has something to do with the last run I went on.

Oh yeah, speaking of which, I haven't run since that night. In fact, now that I think about it, I'm too scared to.

I wonder if these dreams have something to do with that bright light…

December 18th, 2016

Now I'm sure something weird is going on. It isn't just the dreams anymore; now I hear voices when I'm awake. They're inaudible, and in a language I can't quite understand. Like the person in the background when you're on the phone with someone, you can hear the murmur of the voice but can't always make out exactly what they're saying.

It's not my voice. I don't know how to explain it, but I just know it's not.

I was sitting in third period, trying to pay attention to Mrs. Graham droning on about the Revolutionary War, when I thought the kid behind me was whispering something in my ear. I even turned to look at him, and saw it wasn't him because he was too busy drawing a pretty awesome picture of a G.I. Joe.

I turned back, thinking it must've been someone else trying to get another person's attention. Then a few seconds later I heard it again. It was raspy and sounded almost like a growl. I snapped my head around quicker this time, determined to catch the person in the middle of the act, to no avail.

Then I kept hearing it all throughout Mrs. Graham's lecture, and when she didn't chastise anyone—not even the bad kids that sit in the back of the classroom—I knew it was me. I knew it was in my head.

I tried to ignore it, but then I kept hearing it all day.

I think maybe I should tell my mom, but then I think maybe they'll just send me to some loony bin. It might be better to just keep it to myself for a while.

December 20th, 2016

I haven't seen Madeline since I came back from Aunt Cathy's. When I was there I called her a couple of times, but other than that we've both been too busy for each other.

So tonight I called her up, and we went to a movie. We made out a little because the movie kind of sucked.

The entire time the voice whispered in my head. I'm starting to understand bits and pieces of it. It's still mostly inaudible, but I'd say every tenth word or so transmits through.

The word I kept hearing repeated in the message was "Give." I don't know what that means, but Christmas is right around the corner, so maybe it's telling me to give good presents.

How's that for humor?

December 22nd, 2016

There's more going on now than just the voice. The skin on my forearms is slightly raised, like there's something underneath it trying to poke out. If I touch it with my fingers, it feels cold to the touch. Good thing it's the middle of winter so I can wear long sleeves to cover this up.

It's unsightly, but I think it might just be some sort of allergic reaction. I was thinking about telling my mom about it, but then Zeb told me not to.

Oh, Zeb is the voice in my head, remember? The one that told me to "give"? I can understand him pretty good now. I've even tried talking back to him, but whatever means he's using to communicate with me is a one-way only, and instead I just listen to him.

He gives me advice on things, like on how to cover up what's going on with the bumps on my skin. The first rule is to not tell my mom, that would be bad, that would make Zeb's superiors angry.

Zeb says he's in charge of me, and if I mess this up, then I effectively end his life. He asked me if I would feel bad if he was killed.

I laid in my bed with my eyes open, looking at the ceiling above me, wondering why no one ever inspects the spot they spend eight hours a night sleeping under. It could be on the verge of collapsing on top of you, but no one ever bothers to check, they just take it for granted that it doesn't kill them while they sleep.

On top of that, I thought about my answer to Zeb's question. My answer is yes; I would feel bad if Zeb was killed because I didn't comply. I never met Zeb, but I feel as if Zeb is a part of me. I can sometimes feel this heartbeat next to my own heartbeat, like an extra pulse, and I think it's Zeb's.

He lives inside of me, and it's great, because now that me and Zeb are one, I'm never alone.

December 25th, 2016

Merry Christmas. I got a puppy. I named him Charles.

December 29th, 2016

It's bitter cold outside, so damn cold that I can barely stand it. But Zeb told me to go outside tonight and wave up at the stars. He'd be able to see me from where he is, and he told me to imagine him waving back down to me.

Zeb is like the older brother I never had.

I think I love Zeb.

January 3rd, 2017

Last night I couldn't sleep. Zeb's voice has been replaced by a constant buzzing, like machinery whining. It woke me up, and so I took out the journal and thought I'd read it since the last few days—no scratch that—since the last few weeks have been pretty fuzzy.

It's weird that I wrote that I love Zeb, because I'm not even entirely sure if Zeb is even real. It feels like there's something growing inside of me like a parasite. I can kind of feel it squirming, but it's more like something that's living in my mind rather than in my flesh and bones.

I think Zeb is something that's implanted by whatever is inside of me, but what do I know.

I weighed myself this morning. 220 lbs.

I gained weight since that run. Speaking of that run, maybe I should write what happened…

Oh, the whining in my head stopped just now. That's good.

Hey! Zeb is back. Guess I'll write about the run some other time. He's telling me stuff that's important I better pay attention to. Gonna go now.

January 10ᵗʰ, 2017

I'm not sure what's going on with Zeb, but he stopped communicating with me all week. No machinery sound, nothing. It feels like when Madeline dumped me a couple of weeks ago because she said I was acting strange all of a sudden.

Acting strange? I think she was just jealous of Zeb.

Of course, I didn't tell her about Zeb, but I alluded to her that I had another 'friend.'

But really, Zeb is more like family. Man, I miss Zeb.

January 11ᵗʰ, 2017

Now I hear static in my head on and off, but overall it's not distracting. The whining was much worse, and I can feel my thoughts getting clearer and clearer with each passing minute. Zeb seems to be gone, and I don't feel sad about it anymore. I feel more of an emptiness than sadness.

But it's good, because now I'm not sharing my mind with anyone, so I can write freely. I'm finally going to sit down and write about what happened the night I went on a run while visiting Aunt Cathy.

I had my earbuds in, running to Nirvana's *Nevermind*, enjoying the run despite the lashing cold wind and the burn in my muscles. Fifteen minutes into the run and I feel my body getting back into it, start feeling the groove as they say.

I'm going through the dark roads. They wind and bend, and I follow them. It's kind of scary, running at night down countryside roads, there's a certain aura of danger in the still night. Like a murdering scarecrow might burst out of the cornfields and chase me at any moment. Or that I might run into a monster at any turn.

It was kind of fun, until the weird thing that happened next.

A beam of light shot down at me. It was bright blue, like I was caught in the middle of a lightning bolt, except there was no charge to it, harmless besides the brightness. But I was so startled by it that I stopped jogging and looked to see where it was coming from.

My first thought was a searchlight from a helicopter, thinking that my Aunt and Mom woke up in the middle of the night and called the police to come out looking for me or something, but that idea was quickly erased.

The vehicle—Oh Jesus, dare I even write this down? —the spaceship that the beam of light was coming from wasn't like the ones you see on the Syfy Channel or anything like that. It looked more like a hot air balloon, and if I hadn't been directly underneath it, I would've thought that's exactly what it was. But from where I stood, I could see that it wasn't as bloated as a hot air balloon. This thing was flatter.

There wasn't much to it except sleek metal. No insignias, no other lights besides the giant curtain of light I was basked in. A hatch on the bottom of the spaceship slid open, and I began to feel light-headed.

Suddenly the undercarriage of the spacecraft grew bigger and bigger, and I stood there mesmerized by it. It loomed closer to me, and I grew more lightheaded the closer the spaceship came to me.

I looked away, looked down to try to regroup, and realized the ship wasn't coming toward me; it was the other way around. I was going toward *it*. I was suspended in the air. The treetops were several feet below me.

The light got brighter as I went up, and pretty soon I went from squinting my eyes to having to outright close them.

Then, I felt the heaviness of my mass or whatever return to my body and my feet touch solid ground. But before I could even think of moving I felt a pair of hands grab me by the shoulders and force me down onto a bed.

More hands grabbed me when I was lying down. The fingers were cold and slimy, like thin pieces of raw chicken, but their grips were firm and held me from being able to move. The hands grabbed me by the ankles and arms, and then I felt leather straps tighten around my limbs.

I thought about screaming, but I think I was at a point of shock where my vocal chords weren't responding or something because I couldn't scream—only think about it.

A needle went into my arm, and my eyelids shut closed. Then my mind did, as well.

Now that I'm writing this, I know where that dream of the aliens doing surgery on me is coming from, and why it came only after I started hearing Zeb's voice. Because Zeb was in the spaceship that abducted me, or at the very least, he knows the people who were on that spaceship.

He's one of them, I'm absolutely sure of that.

After they sedated me, I don't know how long it was until I woke up, but I was on an operating table. The room was dim except for a light high in the air beaming down on me like a stage light. Just like in the dreams I've been having, there were two shadowed figures hovering above me, staring down at me. In that moment I understood what the animals at the zoo felt like.

I couldn't make out their features from where they were, but I could tell their heads were wide and block-like. The total opposite of the figures in my dream.

The part that the dream had right was that my lips were sewn shut, because now my vocal chords strained, but all I heard was muffled cries trapped behind my shut lips. I tried moving, but I could barely squirm.

The aliens began to communicate with one another, in a language I couldn't understand, but sounded human. It wasn't bleeps and bloops like the movies would have you think. It sounded like a language you'd find on our planet, like something the people in Scandinavia or Bavaria speak.

One of the figure's arms reached out over my head. The arm was thick and broad. Something behind me clicked on, and the arm returned past my vision.

"The translator seems to be malfunctioning lately," the figure that had extended its arm over me said to the other one.

The other figured shrugged. "We'll have to get Clive to look at it when we're done. This is the last one."

"Oh, it is?"

"Mhm, then we can finally go back home."

The figure stretched its arms out and yawned. I heard something crack, its back or in its arms, maybe. "Thank God, Thank God. I miss my bed."

"Oh look, he's awake," the first voice said, and then leaned in closer to me.

I could see its features—no, her features.

Just like the Syfy channel gets the depiction of spaceships wrong, it also gets the depictions of aliens wrong, too. Her features were human, so human I could have been fooled if I didn't remember getting beamed up into the spacecraft. That, and also if her head and face weren't so wide.

Her hair was tied back in a tight bun, and was frizzy like she had been wearing a hat recently. Her eyes were light blue, and the eyebrows above them were as bright red as the hair on her head. It was like seeing a human whose features had been put through a photo editor, stretched out and turned up in brightness.

The mundanity of the sight was scary in its own way, like looking at the funhouse mirror version of the human race.

The woman snapped her fingers in front of my eyes, and I blinked. She grinned in satisfaction.

"Responsive." She said. "Can you hear me?"

I nodded.

I heard the second figure scribbling something on a notepad, and then lean in closer to look at me as well. He looked almost identical to her, could've been twins for all I know. Same fiery red hair, same bright blue eyes.

"You are End-Bringer #32. Do you understand what that means?" The male alien asked me.

I shook my head.

He smiled and then winked at me. "Didn't think so. But you will, when the time is right—"

"If their moderators don't mess it up and make us look bad," the woman alien said, the grin turned into a slyer grin when she said this.

The male alien nodded and then to her said, "Right."

Then to me, "You're probably scared and wondering what's going on."

I tried saying yes, but my lips wouldn't move, so instead I nodded again.

The male alien touched my arm with a hand that felt human but was cold as stone. "Don't worry, when you remember this encounter, you'll be thankful. We're giving you purpose. Making you a part of something greater."

I felt a needle hit my arm. Before I dozed off, I strained my neck to look down at my body. There were towels covering me, but I was naked underneath them, and on top of the towels I could see my blood had bled through the fabric.

I went to sleep, and that's the last I remember of being abducted.

When I woke up, I was back on the dark road, and running again with a lapse in time I couldn't quite figure out. At the time I explained it to myself as just jogger's high, that I had gotten into the "zone" of the run so much that I blanked out and hit a new level of my stride.

I guess Zeb's communications with me jogged my memory. Turns out there was more to that night than I remembered because when I first started writing this entry, I was just going to write about losing track of time after seeing the bright light.

Reliving that took a lot out of me just now. I'm going to go rest.

January 15th, 2017

I'm back down to 200 lbs., hurray! But what I'm actually going to write about is this weird stuff growing out of my arms. I don't think I'll be able to hide them much longer. The blades broke through my skin a few days ago while I was asleep, and in the morning I woke up to my bedsheets covered in blood.

Needless to say, I threw them out and replaced them without anyone in my house noticing me doing it. I'm not sure what these things mean, but they look kind of cool.

They make me feel like Wolverine but with blades.

Zeb is back and talking to me.

[*A second entry on the same date was entered on a separate page in the journal*]

Well, I can't sleep again, and these thoughts have been racing through my mind. Writing seems to be becoming my therapy, and this damn journal seems to be my only friend.

Zeb's been talking to me all day. He's been telling me about myself, more than I care to know. Somehow he knows that the blades on my arms are coming out, and he keeps reassuring me that this is good, that I'm "almost ready."

Almost ready for what? I don't know, I wish I could ask him.

But I have an idea of what's going on now. Those aliens that abducted me, they cut me open and implanted something inside of me. Nanobots or a parasite or some crap like that, and Zeb can somehow communicate with me through whatever they planted in me. He also must have a monitor on my body that informs him of the "phase" we're on, because he knows *everything*.

He apologized one time while I was going number two in the morning. I guess there's a camera on his end, and he said sorry for invading my privacy. Kind of cool and weird at the same time that someone who's potentially lightyears away can spy on me, huh?

Yeah, on second thought, that's not cool at all. I'm getting sleepy. Good night, Journal.

January 17th, 2017

Remember how I said I felt like Wolverine but with blades? Well, this morning I skipped school and went out into the woods behind my house. Zeb taught me how to retract and extract the blades on my command. I'm even more like Wolverine now.

January 20th, 2017

Last night is the last time I'll ever see Madeline.

Actually, last night is the last time anyone'll ever see Madeline.

I haven't talked to her in over a week, but she called me and asked me to hang out last night. So I went over to her house. She was alone, and Zeb told me it was time I give in.

I had no idea what he was talking about, until the impulse to rip her throat out spread through me like a fever.

I cut her head off with the blades on my arms. It was a clean cut, and her head tumbled through her living room floor. It's going to take a lot of carpet spotter to get that stain out.

You can't see it, but I'm laughing right now. And I know that's wrong, but there's a part of me that also doesn't care.

I was made to do this, I was made to kill.

I know because Zeb tells me.

January 21st, 2017

The police took me in to question me about Madeline's death. It was like I wasn't in control of my body or my mind at all, Zeb took over and answered everything for me. He did it perfectly too, convinced the cops that I was innocent and made them feel bad for accusing a 16-year-old boy of killing his girlfriend.

He even made me cry at one point, but I wasn't sad at all. In fact, I felt nothing the entire time they were interrogating me, but my face moved to make the appropriate expressions when Zeb told it to.

Furrowed brows when I was angry at them for asking me what I was doing over her house when her parents weren't over.

"Come on, you were young once," I said to the police, and that was enough of an answer for them.

Followed by surprise, then sadness when they broke the news to me that she had been murdered.

I broke into a sobbing cry after I finally accepted that I would never see her again. It was a performance for the ages.

Sometimes I wonder if Zeb is evil, or if I'm evil. That's when Zeb tells me that science can't be put into such binary boundaries. There is no evil or good in science, only the method.

I think I kind of understand what he means, but not exactly.

I'm a fucking human, Zeb, not your lab monkey.

January 22ⁿᵈ, 2017

On second thought, maybe I am Zeb's lab monkey.

January 25ᵗʰ, 2017

I had another nightmare last night. This time it wasn't about aliens though, this time it was about me being Wolverine. The real Wolverine—well, not the real Wolverine, but me as the real Wolverine. Me with claws, is what I mean to say.

I was in the backyard watching my neighbor's 8-year-old son, Ralphie, through the fence that separates our yards. He was playing with Power Rangers, and I couldn't take my eyes off of the Red Ranger that he kept flinging around and bashing the other toys with. It was like something inside my mind… something buried deep inside, was getting pissed off.

So I used my claws to slash the fence open and ran after Ralphie. Ralphie turned to say hi when he heard me coming, then screamed for a second or two before I slashed his stomach open. I grabbed his dead body and then slammed it against the ground and kicked it across the yard.

Then I came home, took a shower, and drank chocolate milk until it was bedtime.

January 30th, 2017

Turns out my dream had some truth to it. Ralphie was brutally murdered last night. Had his stomach cut open with blades, the police are saying.

I checked to make sure the fence in our yard wasn't slashed open. It wasn't.

But I found a bunch of bloody clothes in a corner of my closet this morning. I'm not sure what that means.

Tomorrow is trash day, I'll just toss the clothes in there.

February 3rd, 2017

I had the same dream about Ralphie. Zeb tells me not to worry about it, but I know something is up.

That dream means something. It means something the way the dreams of the aliens abducting me meant something before.

February 4th, 2017

I killed Ralphie.

Whatever is in my head is what's making me do this. How many more people am I going to kill, Zeb? Huh? How many more before your sick mind is satiated, huh?

I don't think that Zeb and what's inside of me are the same entity. I think that Zeb is just watching me and making sure I fulfill my purpose on this planet. The thing inside of me—whatever it is—is becoming a part of me.

I'm going to cut myself open until I find whatever is inside of me making me do this stuff. I don't want to harm anyone anymore.

Not today though, I'm too tired to do it today. Huh, weird… I don't know why I got tired all of a sudden. I think Zeb is making me gro[ggy(?)]

February 5th, 2017

I tried cutting out whatever is inside of me, but it didn't work. Zeb somehow stopped me from cutting myself open. I held my blade an inch from my stomach, and that's it, it wouldn't move. There was a force field stopping me, I think.

Maybe it wasn't Zeb at all that was stopping me, though. Maybe I just didn't want to do it because I'm starting to realize my purpose.

In fact, Zeb is gone from my mind. So is the static. It's just my thoughts now, and I think I'm starting to figure it all out.

February 7th, 2017

I remember last year I took a philosophy course. We talked about Plato and Socrates and some other guys with too much time on their hands that would sit around pondering about the purpose of life and whatnot.

Well, I'm pondering the same question now. More specifically, I'm pondering the purpose of humankind. What is the point of us? Supposedly we're destroying the planet, right? That's what the scientists on TV say, that's what Zeb used to say when he was still around. Man, I kind of miss him, it's kind of lonely without him peeking in on me while I sit on the toilet.

Just kidding, that's gross.

But back to the purpose of life, really, what is the point of humankind?

As an individual, I know what my purpose is. I *was* just a kid going to Riverton High School that was overweight and always picked last when we played basketball in PE. But now I know I'm so much more than that.

My parents are dead. I killed them last night while they watched TV. It was easy, killing someone. In the movies, they always make it seem like a struggle, that's Hollywood, I guess, but in real life, you just go up to them and cut their heads off. No one expects it, no one fights it.

In fact, my mom's severed head is still smiling from when she saw me approaching her. Dad, I ended his life while he slept. He didn't even open an eye while I killed mom.

Anyway, there's a mountain on the outskirts of town. I've never been there, but I know there's a shuttle bus that takes you there from the bus station because the Boy Scouts take it for their trips up there. There's something on that mountain waiting for me.

I know this, because just like I know everything else, whatever Zeb and his friends put inside of me is telling me this.

See, I thought it was Zeb that was all-knowing at first, but now I know that it's me that knows everything. That's why they abducted me, the aliens, because they knew whatever they had needed a host that would cultivate it, nurse it, give it purpose.

That host was me. See, *I* picked *them*, and they don't even know it.

Anyway, tomorrow I will go to the top of the mountain and realize my purpose.

February 8ᵗʰ, 2017

I am here, and this will be my last entry in this journal. I'm going to throw it down the mountain, but I doubt anyone will find it. I can see the spacecraft waiting for me in the distance. It looks a lot like the one my slaves used to beam me up on their first visit to this doomed planet. The only big difference is there's a giant machine attached to the bottom of it.

When I stand underneath it, the thing inside of me will activate, and this whole planet will be dead. I'm not really sure what the machine on the spacecraft will do, if it blows up the planet then no one will ever read these words, but I have a feeling I'm going to get more weapons on my body and I'll go around killing people.

Hold on. Charlie is at my feet, nipping at my pant leg because he's hungry. I'm going to go feed him and then finish this entry.

Okay, I'm back.

These entries started out as a journal about a fat kid's struggles to lose weight. I wish I could tell all of the fat kids out there that they shouldn't worry about their weight because everything is about to come to an end.

It might appear like a killing spree at first, but nope, it'll be something on a much wider scale. I'm bringing the apocalypse to this planet. One by one, I will slaughter mankind. The end-bringer is here, and I cannot be stopped.

[End of Jeremy Strickland's journal entries]

Afterword

As far as I know, the Ancient Egyptian item that Walter uses to control his army of rodents in *Rodent God* isn't real. I originally wrote it that way and then researched after. I had no luck finding any artifact that the Egyptians believed could control rodents (or animals in general), but I kept it anyway because I liked the layer of mysticism it added to the story.

If there were moments in this anthology that creeped you out, made you sad, or scared you, just imagine having these stories live in your head.

Acknowledgements

First and foremost, I want to thank Laura and Derrick for their endless support. And for lending me their ears when I needed to pitch an idea, or complain. Without you two, I would have lost my damn mind.

A special thanks to Janice and Jonathon for being awesome.

I also would like to thank my editor, David Yost, for giving my sentences liposuction and for the great notes and feedback.

Thanks to all of the guys at GraciePhila. You guys showed me love and support when I put my first book out, and I'll never forget that.

But I especially want to give a very special thanks to my Brazilian jiu-jitsu instructor, Joe. He believes in each and every person who comes through his gym doors, and that includes me. The lessons he teaches go well beyond the mats, and without the discipline I learn from his instructions, these stories would still just be Word documents sitting in my laptop.

And of course, I want to thank each and every person who picked this book up and read it. Even if you hated every word, I sincerely mean this, thank you.

–S. Gomez 12/20/2016

If you enjoyed *Dark Treasures*, you won't want to miss Sergio's debut novel, *The Chaos!*

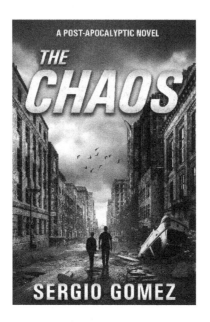

Available on Kindle for $1.99, and at Amazon.com for $8.99

Made in United States
Orlando, FL
16 March 2022